Hastings George Fitzhardinge Berkeley

Japanese Letters

Eastern Impressions of Western Men and Manners...

Hastings George Fitzhardinge Berkeley

Japanese Letters
Eastern Impressions of Western Men and Manners...

ISBN/EAN: 9783337168339

Printed in Europe, USA, Canada, Australia, Japan

Cover: Foto ©Raphael Reischuk / pixelio.de

More available books at **www.hansebooks.com**

JAPANESE LETTERS:

EASTERN IMPRESSIONS

OF

WESTERN MEN AND MANNERS,

AS CONTAINED IN THE CORRESPONDENCE OF

TOKIWARA AND YASHIRI.

EDITED BY

COMMANDER HASTINGS ⌐BERKELEY, R.N.,

AUTHOR OF "WEALTH AND WELFARE."

———

.

LONDON:
JOHN MURRAY, ALBEMARLE STREET.

NEW YORK:
LONGMANS, GREEN, & CO.
1891.

PREFACE.

In the past few years much has been written by Europeans, especially by Englishmen, concerning Japan and the Japanese. Moreover, that which has been written has been eagerly read. There is in this nothing surprising. The originality and excellence of Japanese art—particularly of Japanese decorative design—copied, disseminated, and, as usual in parallel cases, now vulgarised among us, have stimulated the slow curiosity of the public concerning this people,—a curiosity which, in inquiring minds, has grown the more lively on account of the remarkable experiment which the Japanese nation has so thoroughly, and, thus far, so successfully conducted : nothing less than that of breaking up its ancient civilisation and recasting the fragments thereof in a European mould.

After having heard and read so much about Japan and its people from Europeans, it may prove interesting to hear what Japanese themselves have to say about Europe and Europeans in relation to this metamorphosis of the laws, customs and political institutions of their country.

It must be admitted that a collection of private letters, written by persons who do not stand prominently in the public eye, should possess intrinsic merit, or unusual interest of some kind, in order to deserve publication. Some interest there almost always is in the impressions, appreciations and judgments of individuals whose manner of life and ways of thought are not ours : perhaps no less, indeed, in those of individuals whose persistent endeavour it has been to adapt themselves to this manner and walk in these ways. Whether there is in these letters interest sufficient to engage and retain the reader's attention is matter for him or his " taster "—detestable but expressive word—to determine.

As a mere translator and editor of others' work, I might have permitted myself, without incurring the charge of fatuity or vanity, to say a few words in its praise, to touch on its points of utility, interest, humour or other excellence. I have not done so : for reasons which the intelligent reader will not find it difficult to guess, and with which the unintelligent reader need not be troubled.

Matters which are merely of domestic interest to the writers of these letters, or which relate to their private affairs, have been excluded from the translation ; that only has been retained which appeared to possess general interest. In the process of translation certain surface peculiarities have disappeared of themselves, others have been toned down purposely. If something of the flavour of the original has thus been lost, a more than countervailing advantage has been gained, for peculiarities which are entertaining merely because they are strange or uncommon become tiresome by repetition. But for this word of explanation the ingenious reader might almost have suspected the writers of the following letters to be children of the editor's imagination.

H. B.

CONTENTS.

LETTER I.

PAGE

TOKIWARA TO HIS FRIEND YASHIRI :—Arrival at Aden
—Impressions—Steamer Point; Its Origin and For-
tuitous Appearance—Effect, on Surface Habits, of
Change in Mode of Life 1

LETTER II.

TOKIWARA TO YASHIRI :—Suez—Individual Distinctions and Racial Characteristics—The Red Sea :
Victims of Civilisation—The Law of Competition :
"Free Contract between Men" or "Contract between Free Men"?—Agrarian Riots in Japan . . 7

LETTER III.

TOKIWARA TO YASHIRI :—Cairo—Egypt the Wonderful—The Pyramids and Burial Grounds—An Idea
of Death : Its Embodiment and Influence on the
Life and Aims of a People—Natural Development
of the Egyptian System of Sepulture and Mortuary
Art—Change of Method, but Identity of Aim, as
the Sceptre passes from Memphis to Thebes . . 12

LETTER IV.

TOKIWARA TO YASHIRI :—At Sea—The Sacrilegious
Hand of the Egyptologist—*Jomard's* Description of
the Pyramids—England's Power and Pre-eminence . 19

LETTER V.

PAGE

TOKIWARA TO YASHIRI :—Malta—Its Harbours and
their Pictorial Effect—The English and the Maltese
—Subject Races and their Masters—Necessary Political Servitude 24

LETTER VI.

TOKIWARA TO YASHIRI :—At Sea—An Ideal Mediter-
ranean Day—Modern Thought and Poetical Beliefs
—Life on Board Ship—Energy and Englishmen—An
Amiable Bore—Gibraltar 28

LETTER VII.

TOKIWARA TO YASHIRI :—London—First and Confused Impressions—Pekin and London—Aspect of
the Population—Intellectual Activity—Dissimilarity
in Social Aggregates and its Surface Effects—London
Dwellings—Industrialism and Ideals of Beauty . 35

LETTER VIII.

YASHIRI TO TOKIWARA :—Philosophy and Sentiment
—The World and the Suffering therein—Competi-
tion : Friendly and Unfriendly—Knowledge and the
Power of Sympathy—The Lesson of Egypt—The
Irony of Fate 41

LETTER IX.

YASHIRI TO TOKIWARA :—The Intellectual Indifferent-
ism of Young Japan—Belief and Prejudice—The
Practical Man of Action—Intellectual Gyrations
and Subtleties—The Adroit Gymnast—The Weariness of Uncertainty 46

LETTER X.

YASHIRI TO TOKIWARA:—The Malady of Thought—
Fatalism—Free-will—Young Japan and Stable
Reform—Ideals of Life—The Fruits of Agnosticism 51

. LETTER XI.

PAGE

TOKIWARA TO YASHIRI :—The Middle Class in Europe
—Upper and Lower Classes in England—The Sar-
torial Art—Feminine Adornments—Tailors and
Jews—The Influence of Dress. 57

LETTER XII.

YASHIRI TO TOKIWARA :—Reforms and Reformers—
Necessity of Belief—How to Attain a Comforting
and Comfortable Belief—The Way of the Un-
believer--Impotence of Unbelief 64

LETTER XIII.

TOKIWARA TO YASHIRI :—Constitutional Government
—The Queen and the Mikado—English Common-
sense—The Anglican Church—The Christian
Churches 69

LETTER XIV.

YASHIRI TO TOKIWARA :—The Travelling Politician—
Eastern Problems and Western Ideals—A Defence
of Harakiri—Western Prejudice in the Matter of
Suicide 74

LETTER XV.

TOKIWARA TO YASHIRI :—The Plebeian Sovereigns of
the West—Influence of the British Sovereign on
Morals and Manners—Morality and Hypocrisy—
The Impurities of Social Life—The English Middle
Class—Industrialism as a Cause of the Revolution
of Mediæval Society 79

LETTER XVI.

YASHIRI TO TOKIWARA :—English Newspapers: *The
Times* in its Capacity of Universal Critic—Ver-
satile and Mimetic Character of the Japanese—Japan
as an " England of the East " 85

LETTER XVII.

PAGE

TOKIWARA TO YASHIRI :—The Western Spirit of Inquiry—Accessibility of English Society—Hospitality
—The *Abord* of the Average Englishman—The
Houses of Parliament—Westminster Abbey—Independence and Courtesy 90

LETTER XVIII.

YASHIRI TO TOKIWARA :—The Splenetic Condition—
The Too Practical European—Happiness in Acqui-
sition or in Acquisitiveness ?—Topsy-turvydom of
European Methods—Pride of Possession and the
Artistic Sense. 96

LETTER XIX.

TOKIWARA TO YASHIRI :—Paris : Compared with
London—The English and the French Press—
Society in France and in England—The Way of
the Paris Artisan—Tradition, Empiricism, and
Shallow Logic—The Road to Happiness . . 102

LETTER XX.

YASHIRI TO TOKIWARA :—Men and Constitution-
mongers—The Humours of Parliamentary Government—The Political Puppet-show—The Relation
between Facts and Party Discipline, as Exemplified
in the Political Press 108

LETTER XXI.

TOKIWARA TO YASHIRI :—*Liberté, Egalité, Fraternité*—
Men, or Marionettes ?—" Equal Inalienable Rights "
—Equality of Men before the Law—Individualism
in Europe 113

LETTER XXII.

PAGE

YASHIRI TO TOKIWARA :—Japan's Too Ardent Party of
Progress—Promulgation of the New Constitution—
The Houses of Representatives—Lack of a Middle
Class—Test of Popular Fitness for Representative
Institutions 119

LETTER XXIII.

TOKIWARA TO YASHIRI:—The Art of Polite Conver-
sation in French Society—In English Society—
Social Qualities of Frenchmen and Englishmen—
Distinctions between the English " Upper Ten
Thousand " and the French " Beau Monde "—The
Freemasonry of Fashion in England . . . 125

LETTER XXIV.

TOKIWARA TO YASHIRI :—Rome—The Religious Centre
of the Western World—The Pope and Temporal
Power—Claims of Christianity as a Religion for the
Japanese—Christianity and Monotheism. . . 131

LETTER XXV.

YASHIRI TO TOKIWARA :—Japanese Reform and the
Foreign Colony in Japan—Pretensions of the
Foreigners—False Estimate of Japanese Character
—Appreciations of the Foreign Press—Philosophy :
" Cheap and Nasty " 136

LETTER XXVI.

TOKIWARA TO YASHIRI :—Reflections on the Origin and
Development of the Christian Religion : The God
of the Hebrews : The Jews in the Time of Christ :
The Teaching of Christ : The Building up of Dogma
—The Nature of the Deity 142

LETTER XXVII.

PAGE

YASHIRI TO TOKIWARA:—The Japanese Student Riots
in 1888—Latitudinarianism in Morality—Morality
in the Abstract and Man in the Concrete—The
" Advanced Young Person" on Morality and Convention—The Right and the Wrong of Moral
Precepts 150

LETTER XXVIII.

TOKIWARA TO YASHIRI:—The Trinity in Unity: A
Scientific Illustration—The "Fatal Facility" of the
Polytheistic Idea—Interpretation of Dogma in the
Roman Catholic Church—The Church and the Indi-
vidual 156

LETTER XXIX.

YASHIRI TO TOKIWARA:—The Fortuitous Application
of the Modern Theory of Evolution to Human Progress—How Abuse of Words leads to Abuse of
Things—Opportunism in Morals 161

LETTER XXX.

TOKIWARA TO YASHIRI:—The Christian Churches—
Characteristics of the Roman Catholic and the Pro-
testant—Race and Religion in the East and West—
The Shaping of Abstract Ideals to Practical Ends
—Protestantism as a Religion for Japan . . 166

LETTER XXXI.

YASHIRI TO TOKIWARA :—Are the Rich Growing Richer
and the Poor Poorer ?—Concomitants of Modern
Industrial Organisation—Development of Industry
and the Line of Demarcation between Rich and
Poor—The Elysium of Riches and the Hell of
Poverty 174

Contents.

LETTER XXXII.

PAGE

TOKIWARA TO YASHIRI :—London Again—The Land of Business—Capital and Credit—What is a Capitalist? —Credit and its Manipulation by Capitalists and Bankers—Commercial Crises and Panics—Rise and Establishment of the Modern Plutocracy . . . 181

LETTER XXXIII.

TOKIWARA TO YASHIRI :—The Jews—Prescience of the Hebrew Prophets—Advance of the Jews on the Flowing Tide of Industrialism—The Jew Before the Industrial Era, and After—Shakespeare in the Mouth of Shylock—The Jewish Record . . . 188

LETTER XXXIV.

YASHIRI TO TOKIWARA :—Educational Value of the Novel—Authentic Documents for Posterity—The French Realistic School—The Biographer and the Novelist—Young Japan and the Form and Spirit of the West 197

LETTER XXXV.

TOKIWARA TO YASHIRI :—Progress and Conservation— The Comedy of Politics—Origin, Development, and Transformation of English Political Parties—The Irish Question—A Transcendental System of Morality in Embryo—Possibility of its Development— Means to this End 202

LETTER XXXVI.

YASHIRI TO TOKIWARA :—Religion and Temperament —Religion and the Masses—Life and its Problems —Genius and Judgment—Racial Dissimilarities— Revolutionary Reform 213

LETTER XXXVII.

PAGE

TOKIWARA TO YASHIRI:—Art and Vulgarity—The
Western Sense of Beauty in Art--Western Apprecia-
tion of Japanese Art—The Instinct and Power of
Imitation—Art in Japan and in England. . . 219

LETTER XXXVIII.

YASHIRI TO TOKIWARA:—A Foreign Visitor—Western
Appreciations of Native Customs—Feminine Adornments—Paints and Cosmetics—The Natural and
the Artificial 225

LETTER XXXIX.

TOKIWARA TO YASHIRI:—The Albert Hall and
Memorial—Symbolism in Art—The Musical Public
—Art and the British Public—Adaptation of De-
corative Design 229

LETTER XL.

YASHIRI TO TOKIWARA:—Socialistic Bias of the Japanese People—Individualism and Socialism—Power
and Responsibility—The Power of the Purse in
Modern Life—The Direction and Control of Labour 235

LETTER XLI.

TOKIWARA TO YASHIRI:—The Art of Advertising—The
Vulgarisation of Religion—Tract Societies and the
Salvation Army—The Religious and the Artistic
Sense—Religion, Morality, and Art . . . 244

LETTER XLII.

TOKIWARA TO YASHIRI:—The Japanese in Search of a
Religion, of a Basis of Morality—Reform in Japan
—Mobility and Versatility of the Japanese Mind
—The Luxury of Ideas—Ideologists and Men of
Business 250

JAPANESE LETTERS.

LETTER I.

TOKIWARA TO HIS FRIEND YASHIRI.

ADEN, *August* 30*th*, 1888.

WE arrived here early this morning, in oppressive splendour of weather. Now, as I write, it is late in the afternoon, and I make profit of the shiftless hour before weighing anchor to send you a line or two about Aden—or rather (for you can find out all about Aden in the geography books) a reflexion of the dominant Aden-mood in me.

A chain of mountainous rock, bare, brown and contorted, frowning savagely over a wilderness of sand and sea: such is Aden. Rarely, if ever, have my eyes rested on, or rather brooded over— for here is no true rest—a site more desolate and forbidding. In the wild, waste places of the earth there are doubtless many spots yet more inhospitable, more desolate, more forbidding; but usually

10

I

we come upon them expectantly, forewarned, with a mind steeled to look upon them as of the wild and the waste. Here, however, is a dwelling-place of men, a busy port of call, a half-way house between the East and the West, where the distant echoes of two worlds faintly reverberate and mingle. Unprepared for so harsh a contrast between the actual and the imagined, your soft expectant mood comes abruptly to an end with a slight shudder of surprise, from which you do not at once recover.

Over Aden reigns, almost uninterruptedly, a cloudless sky, pure pale blue, very different in its uniformity from the varying and variable tones which overspread our native heavens. A fierce, untempered sun scorches bare the naturally arid hills, pours its pitiless rays over long leagues of yellow sand and blue sea. The heat, the light, the glare strike at you from all sides, from above, from below; from cloudless sky, from burning land and glittering sea: you are sent staggering with a confused impression of the feebleness of man, delicately nurtured, unaided, at odds with the blind physical forces of nature.

The traveller lands at Steamer Point, the port of Aden. Aden itself is at a distance of about one and a half *ri*,[1] out of sight behind the brown hills. You get at it (the insupportable dulness of Steamer Point spurring you to the enterprise, notwithstand-

---

[1] A *ri* is nearly two and a half miles.—Ed.

ing the heat) by climbing some two-thirds of the
way up the rocky range, towards a dip in the line
of summit. Not unnaturally you make up your
mind to a hot and toilsome journey over the dip,
but long before getting to it the unexpected over-
takes you, and this time not unpleasantly, as the
case is too often; for, to your grateful astonishment, you pass, not over the dip but under it,
through a tunnel, at the farther end of which,
emerging from the half-darkness, you look down
upon Aden in a flood of light. There is nothing
in the aspect of it which draws you to a closer
acquaintance, unless it be the novelty of a city
built in the hollow of a low crater, admirably
defended by fortifications. To the right, as you
look Adenward, are the famous water tanks hol-
lowed out of the soil centuries ago by the Arabs.
They lie close up to the mouth of a rocky
ravine, so narrow and steep-sided that the sun illu-
mines its depths for a few minutes only at noon.
I believe it rains here on the average about once
in two or three years. On these rare occasions,
however, the skies tolerate no half-measures, and
the tanks, which contain many more million
gallons than I can remember, are filled to the
brim in less than an hour.

Steamer Point, where, as I said, you land, is not
a town, nor a village, nor an ordinary seaport; nor,
indeed, anything but a seemingly fortuitous con-
course of shipping agencies, marine stores, and

hotels. You would imagine the demon of the
desert, in a sardonic mood, had been at work here.
But in truth the *raison d'être* of Steamer Point has
naught to do with the devil, unless in the form
of an Englishman. Its origin is quite prosaic.
Those earth-hungry, energetic and indefatigable
English seized Aden in 1838. Two or three years
before the abolition of the Shôgunate[1] the Suez
Canal was opened, and thenceforward all the
shipping between the East and the West called
there. In a very short time Steamer Point grew
to be what it now is—not a thing of beauty by any
means. The stores, hotels and agencies are laid
out in a semicircle at the foot of the rocky hill
range, their white fronts staring out to sea over a
sandy flat whose uniform dulness is broken only in
one spot by a wooden shed, beneath the shade
of which lurk two or three very melancholy-look-
ing and broken-down one-horse carriages. Viewed
from the harbour the pictorial effect is more strange
than pleasing. The background is too wild,

[1] The Shôgun, a sort of *maire du palais* to the Mikado,
was the head of the feudal aristocracy or military hierarchy,
i.e., the Buke or Daimiôs—not to be confounded with the
Kuge or court nobility, hereditary officials of the Mikado's
Court. He was for centuries the temporal sovereign of
Japan. The last Shôgun sent in his resignation on November 19th, 1867. This act caused great discontent among
his vassals, and was followed, in 1868, by the civil war which
ended in the restoration of the Mikado to the real headship
of the nation.—ED.

rugged and savagely unconventional for the habita-
tions ; and these wear a timid sheepish look, as if
acknowledging, in deprecatory manner, that amid
such surroundings they have no legitimate place.

It is remarkable with what ease and rapidity
custom can transform our surface habits. To sit
on a chair instead of on the heels, to eat from a
table in the European fashion instead of Japanese-
wise, have become, even in so short a time,
almost familiar, almost natural to me. The sudden change from the solid platform of land to this
willowy-watery stage, arms the senses against
surprises, which, consequently, come upon you un-
surprisingly. You find yourself on this unfamiliar
element, amid strange surroundings, and therefore
grow suddenly watchful. The usual and scarcely
conscious bodily ways and motions become fully
conscious to you, and you yourself circumspect.
So simple and familiar a motion as walking becomes matter for calculation and forethought, and
the safeguarding of crockery (how far more practical
our lacquered woodware in these circumstances !)
at meal-times one not merely for calculation but
for the exercise of manual dexterity—leading, too,
to the yet wholesomer practice of toleration for the
awkwardnesses and bunglings of your immediate
neighbours to right, to left, and especially in front
of you. I need scarcely say that, in order to avoid
attracting the too close attention and the indiscreet
comments of strangers, I am careful to shape my

external ways after those which I observe about me—in all save one, at least: the disgusting European use, or abuse, of the pocket-handker-chief. Nevertheless, customs habitual from infancy occasionally prove too strong for novel ones, especially at those inevitable moments when con-scious attention is relaxed and circumspection falls asleep. More than once, strolling on deck in fine and calm weather, I have sunk somewhat too serenely and securely into meditation, and have awoken therefrom to find myself seated on deck in the manner natural to us—not without surprising, on kindly faces, the flitting away of a gently malicious smile.

LETTER II.

SUEZ, *September 5th*, 1888.

I FEAR you will have been disappointed with my letter from Aden; not perhaps on account of what there is in it (forgive the fatuity), but of what there is not. I have not forgotten my promise that Western men and Western manners—as actually seen, not merely read of—and what we may make of them for our own benefit, are to be the subject-matter of my letters to you. I have not forgotten your last words, those of the classic English poet : "the proper study of mankind is man"; but as yet I have found nothing to say which seems worth the saying. The time has been too short and the opportunities too few. As regards Europeans in general and Englishmen in particular, I am no further forward than when I left home. Individual distinctions still in a great measure baffle and elude me. To note the divergence of racial characteristics is not a very hard matter, but to distinguish the minor and more delicate individual ones is a far more difficult task, and one requiring

7

that familiarity of daily intercourse which soon ripens into easy and unsuspicious commerce.

Our own circle in Tokio possesses, I think, a fairly accurate impression of the characteristic marks of the Potter on the clay of Europe, but the family resemblance of the pipkins is at first sight so overpowering as to daze the senses to any but the most superficial dissimilarities. This experience, of course, is natural enough, and, I suppose, universal. There is an Englishman on board, an old traveller, with whom I have made some sort of acquaintance. We exchanged confidences on the subject. He told me that when he first visited China all the inhabitants, even those with whom he was in daily contact, appeared to him " as like as peas " (and no doubt they were so, and are so even now, if he will but look at peas close enough) not merely in physical appearance, but in cast of mind, general disposition, beliefs, opinions, and tastes—sensitive of feeling and punctilious of honour in respect of some things ; hard, callous and indifferent with regard to others.

It was very hot in the Red Sea : so hot that two firemen died of heat apoplexy. Amid so much which appears the perfection of order, smoothness and the fitness of means to ends, the death of these two men at their work and because of their work came upon me with a depressing sense of surprise. Death, indeed, is the end of life, but it seemed to me that here was something out of joint in the fitness.   The toil and exhaustion which attend the propulsion of these vessels at high speeds through hot and breezeless zones, are certainly in causal relation with such death-strokes—frequent, I am told, among the firemen.   Civilisation has its victims no less surely than barbarism.   Europeans pride themselves, perhaps with justice, on being more careful of human life, more tender and chary of inflicting pain, than we Easterns.   That we should do any better than they in like circumstances I do not venture to assert, but that which Europeans do is, to say nothing else of it, neither careful nor tender.   Careful and tender people, one would suppose, sooner than be even in a remote way the cause of such accidents, would suffer with equanimity the loss of a little time in the carriage of their tender selves and weighty correspondence.   So I mused, and presently, perceiving my acquaintance the Englishman walking about on deck, I put over me a veil of gentle irony, which I imagined would be very effective, and questioned him on the subject.   I was deceived, and yet learnt a lesson.   He did not appear to comprehend or even to notice the irony, and his surprise at my questions was by no means veiled. He did not disguise the fact that he personally had given but little attention to such matters, looking upon them as satisfactorily settled for himself and for the world at large through the demonstrably inevitable action of the laws of competition and supply and demand, laws which I had supposed were accepted merely in an academical sense. Here was an application of theory to practice which opened my eyes to the value of education. You perceive, of course, how the matter stands. First of all, the steamship companies compete with one another for the favour of the public; this they do by running their hardest at the lowest possible prices, and this in its turn entails their getting the greatest amount of work on the lowest possible scale of wages out of the officers, sailors and fire-men in their employ. Then if you take the firemen, or "seedie" boys as they are called, as a further illustration of the principle, the process is much the same : the "seedie" boys compete for employ-ment at the fires on the terms offered by the com-panies, the keenness of competition being regulated by the proportion between the "demand" for services and the "supply." It is all perfectly fair, above-board, and even necessary; based on "free contract between people"—which expression, I rather think, is intended to stand for "contract between free people." In fact, the system resembles a circle of iron necessity, and there is nothing like necessity for keeping people contented. Thus the shareholders of the steamship companies, and the directors, and the officers and the public in general, are quite content; even so are the "seedie" boys, when they do not die, and when they die they have no further care.

The frank, unreserved and general acceptance and recognition of the law of competition as truly governing the relations in which men stand to one another must introduce a sweet simplicity, a smooth celerity of execution in the conduct of men's affairs. By the clear wide-scattered light of this wisdom the evil powers of anarchy and lawlessness must stand at once self-revealed and self-condemned. Thus in Europe, doubtless, such social disorders as the agrarian riots once common among the foolish peasantry of our poorer districts (ignorantly desirous of living, in spite of the laws of political economy) can now find no place.[1] In these days of diseased self-introspection this knowledge must also act as a valuable corrective to the weak and fatuous self-condemnation of the morally invertebrate rich, by assuring them that their possession of the good things of this world is an absolutely rightful possession, that the rich are rich and the poor poor in virtue of a natural law with which it is demonstrably foolish to interfere.

[1] The writer no doubt alludes to the frequent disturbances and serious troubles in the poor agricultural districts of Japan before 1868. These riots were most frequent and dangerous in certain tracts of land owned by the lesser nobles, who, being in constant attendance at the court of the Shôgun, formed a class of absentee landlords.—ED.

LETTER III.

CAIRO, *September* 10*th*, 1888.

I WAS warned not to attempt Cairo or any part of Egypt at this season of the year, but my curiosity outran my discretion, so eager was I to see something of this world-famed country. I left the steamer at Ismailia (in the Suez Canal) and came on here by rail, with the intention of continuing my journey seaward from Alexandria by the following mail-boat. The hotel in which I have taken up my quarters is almost tenantless. I read quietly during the day. or roam about the large deserted rooms, for it is too hot to venture out of doors until sundown. I read about this sun-satiate land, lying there soundless, as if enchanted under the spell of deathless memories.—By the way, I am very glad that I decided to adopt entirely the European costume, and to observe, as nearly as I can, European ways and habits during my absence from home. These precautions have already sheltered me from much of that impertinent curiosity which we, at home, have so often had cause

12

to remark, and resent, in our casual European acquaintances.

I have been here already four days, and yet 1 have done nothing in the way of excursions save two visits by moonlight to the famous pyramids and one to the scarcely less famous city of the dead. But if perforce of heat I have found little time to go about seeing the sights of the land, I have had leisure to read about them, and—what might be done to advantage more frequently—to think of what I read. It is strange, however, seeing what my occupation has been, how often my thoughts have reverted to the incident of those two firemen who died in the Red Sea and are now at the bottom of it—victims rather than benefici-aries (save for the benefit of death) of an advancing civilisation. But doubtless, if we look well into it, the number of those who profit increases faster than the number of those who lose. Certain is it that, under what dispensation soever we live, it is always the strong man who inherits the fulness of the earth, no less than that into this word "strong," time, clime and circumstance force us to read the most disparate meanings.

Two days hence I shall be at Alexandria. I cannot undertake a visit to the temples and palaces, —they are too distant, and the weather is too hot. But, as I said, I have seen the pyramids and the great city of the dead : the pyramids of Cheops, Chephren and Mycerinus, and the vast burial-

ground of ancient Memphis. How full of wonder
it all is!—and, at first, how perplexing! You gaze
on these wondrous relics of the past, so strange to
us in their brutal hugeness, and ask yourself what
lesson is there written for him who will take the
trouble to decipher it? What do they mean? what
is the conception, the idea which they embody?
For even the most insignificant work of man's hand
or tongue is the embodiment, the outward expression of the thought within him. You read and
ponder. At last the light breaks in upon you, and
you stand wonder-struck, well-nigh awe-struck with
the supreme, compelling, shaping power of a mere
abstract theoretical idea over the life of a whole
nation. That a simple, unverifiable conception, a
mere prefigurement of the possible conditions of
a future existence, should move men to works so
colossal and so enduring, is matter for instructive
reflection. I do not overlook the fact that in all
epochs fruitful of great undertakings the " possible
conditions " have always been whole-heartedly,
fervently believed to be the actual, the absolute—
hence, of course, the power of the conception.

In every corner of the habitable globe the idea
of death has been fraught with consequences of
incalculable importance, and has left behind it
memorials of its astounding power. In no spot
of earth, however, has it left memorials of itself,
of its reckless, almost brutal power, so striking as
in this narrow valley, this cradle of the civilisation

of the Western world.   Can you figure to yourself
these pigmies at work in their thousands and tens
of thousands, year after year, decade after decade,
under that ever serene blue sky?   An army of
workers, regiments of labour such as the world
has never since seen, such as in all probability the
world never saw before nor will see again.   What
perseverance, what lordly contempt of difficulties,
what perfection of organisation and discipline do
not these vast structures bear witness to!

And yet, given the initial conception of death
entertained by these Egyptians six or seven
thousand years ago, the development of their
system of sepulture and of their mortuary art,
appears simple, natural, inevitable.   A little more
or a little less spirituality in this conception, and
surely I should not now be gazing in wonder on
these legacies of an unforgotten world.   With the
ancient Egyptian the idea of death was associated
with that of separation between soul and body,
but he could never quite master the conception
of a purely detached spiritual existence as we
do in these days.   I do not mean, of course, that
we can really imagine or picture it to ourselves,
but we can *think* of it, as we think of an infinite
curve or of a point without magnitude.   In the
mind of the Egyptian it was necessary, if the soul
was not to be altogether snuffed out, that it should
find for itself after death a material support of
some kind connected with the body (or, in the

later development of the idea) with the memory
of the dead. The first, most obvious, and most
natural support was the body itself: hence, of
course, the growth of the embalmer's art. But
whatever might be the degree of perfection to
which this art could be carried, it was felt that the
day must come at last when time would claim the
fulfilment of the law in virtue of which all things
are built up and suffer destruction. Thus, in the
regular and logical course of invention, came the
manufacture of those models and statuettes of
the deceased hidden with all imaginable care and
precaution in the mortuary chamber—models and
statuettes which might take the place of the decay-
ing or destroyed body as a resting-place for the
soul. Hence again, by an inevitable development
of ideas, the notion that mural paintings represent-
ing the deceased, his worldly possessions, his daily
occupations, his favourite sports and pastimes,
would establish his memory, and, by favour of the
gods, in a manner re-create these things for him
in the shadowy, indistinct realm of the new life.
Finally it came to be believed that prayers, in
which were specified and recited the presumed
necessities and the once mundane possessions of
the deceased, were of themselves sufficient to
insure to him the enjoyment of these things ; a
whole multitude of priests appear to have been
engaged in the ceaseless daily repetition of such
prayers as part of their priestly duties.

From this general and *a priori* conception that a material support in some way connected with the memory of the dead was necessary for the survival of the soul, we can readily comprehend the importance attached by the Egyptians to the inviolability of the tomb. We need in no way be surprised at the vast amount of labour involved and the ingenuity displayed in the construction of monuments which have served to secure bodies, models, statuettes and mural paintings from the slow injuries of time and from the rapacious and destroying hand of the treasure-seeker. Precisely the same conception, though working under changed conditions, governs the procedure of this people when, at a later date, the seat of empire is removed to Thebes. The physical conformation of the country about Thebes being entirely different from that which surrounds Memphis, the methods used for compassing the inviolability of the dead are changed. Memphis is open to the desert. Thebes is hemmed in by the mountains which, south of the Delta, overlook the valley of the sacred river. To build pyramids in this narrow valley would be entirely useless work, for the mountains themselves will make finer and more secure tombs than any pyramid, not to speak of the difficulties attending the erection of structures so gigantic in the restricted space afforded by the valley. Thus the mountains naturally become the houses of the dead. They are tunnelled out into

2

corridors and chambers, which penetrate far into the bowels of them—hundreds of yards, if I am not mistaken. Incredible is the amount of labour which has been bestowed on these works. Devices of surprising cunning and ingenuity have been employed to mask the entrances to the corridors and to dissemble the position of the real mortuary chamber.

The past history of this land is of absorbing interest to the nations of Europe. For many years now a body of explorers and archæological students known under the name of Egyptologists have been engaged in upturning and ransacking these records of the far past. What I have been telling you is, in thousandfold detail, the common property and knowledge of the many people interested in the results of their labours. The history of Ancient Egypt is indelibly, if obscurely, written in these embodiments of an idea of death, and its secrets, mutely guarded during thousands of years, are now being slowly and surely dragged forth into the light of day.

LETTER IV.

TOKIWARA TO YASHIRI.

AT SEA, *September* 17th, 1888.

IN the flesh I am at sea, on board ship, steaming along the blue Mediterranean; but in the spirit I am yet in Egypt the wonderful, wandering under the silver moon, at the foot of the great pyramid, in and out of the tombs, round about the Sphinx with fateful look.

There is something hallowed and at the same time indescribably sad about these remnants of the past, memorials of long departed generations—a feeling of dismay that even for these stupendous pyramids the day must be when the sun shall rise in the clear morning and behold an empty site, or a populous, but them no longer. Every imagined chip of the hammer on those old stones jars painfully on my inner ear. Indeed, it occurs to me to ask, not altogether in tones of mock indignation, by what kind of right, other than might, those students and explorers ransack tomb, mausoleum and pyramid? I do not speak of the right conferred by the authorities of the country: I

19

refer to the assumed right of violating the express intention, of destroying the assured hope, of these old Egyptians. I ask the question in all seriousness. What greater certainty, or likelihood, is there about any one of our ideas of a future life,—yours, mine, that of the Shintoists, of the Buddhists, of the Moslems, of these Christians, all of them held to with fervent faith, as a sheet-anchor by which to outride the stormy days of life,—that any of us should venture to treat that of these bygone people after so cavalier a fashion ? Picture to yourself what your feelings would have been, as an ancient Egyptian, could you have suspected that presently (for what are four or five thousand years to eternity?) prying strangers, out of mere curiosity, idly, from no reputable desire of revenge, without even the excuse afforded by the hunger for treasure, would calmly, ruthlessly, put an end to the existence of your soul ? Nay, imagine your feelings now, when after forty centuries of honourable seclusion, you find yourself watching, with indignant interest, these nimble-fingered aliens working off your old friends and acquaintances, knowing full well that before long your own turn must come ! Think of it, my friend. I say it most solemnly, most deliberately : these old Egyptians, with their idea of a future life, may be in the right—as much, or as little, as you or I, as a Buddhist, a Moslem, a Christian. If they are in the right, here are we (I mean the explorers) deliberately slaying these poor souls by the thousand. Let the Egyptologists look to it !

I will not give you a description of the Pyramids. You will find in your library better and more accurate notes than any I could give you. But of the effect which they produce on the beholder you may gather a good notion from the following passage, which I transcribe and translate from the pages of a well-known French explorer [1] :—

" The general aspect of these monuments causes a strange impression. Their summits, seen in the distance, appear not unlike the tops of high mountains clear-cut against the sky. The nearer you approach, the more this effect diminishes. When you are within a short distance of these huge symmetrical masses, however, you are affected in quite another way. Surprise and wonder grow in you as you walk up the acclivity above which they stand. At last, when you find yourself actually at the foot of the Great Pyramid, you are seized with a powerful and poignant emotion, tempered by a kind of stupor of bewilderment. Summit and angles are lost to view. What you experience is not the admiration inspired by a great work of art—it is simply a profound but indescribable *impression*. This in the first place springs from the grandeur and simplicity of the object, in the second place from the contrast, the

[1] Jomard, *Description de l'Egypte—Antiquités*, t. v., p. 597.—ED.

disproportion between man's stature and the vast-
ness of this work of his hand. The bodily eye
cannot take it in, that of the imagination itself fails
to grasp it readily. It is by degrees only that you
get an adequate notion of that vast mass of hewn
stone rising symmetrically to so prodigious a height.
Blocks of stone measuring two hundred cubic feet
and weighing fifteen tons apiece are there by the
hundred. There are thousands of others hardly,
if at all, smaller. You touch them, feel them with
your hands, and seek to picture to yourself the
power which quarried, carted, raised, each to its
appointed place, this immense number of colossal
stone blocks ; how many men worked thereat, for
what length of time, what means they used. And
the less distinctly you can imagine these things to
yourself, the more you admire the power which
made sport of such obstacles."

The evidence of England's power and greatness,
especially of her colonial and commercial supremacy, is scattered broadcast about our path. Along
the route which I have been following, the presence,
the influence of England is predominant. Her
power indeed is scattered, but not dissipated.
After leaving the far East, the first place of call is
Aden, and the first thing to be seen there is the
uniform of the English soldier. You leave Aden
to pass through the Straits of Bab-el-Mandeb into
the Red Sea, and find this gateway to Europe in
English hands. You steam through the Suez

Canal, and remember that its banks and the surrounding country are under the protection (read " in
the possession") of England.   Not very far from the
northern end of the Canal these ubiquitous islanders
are again to be found in a "post of observation":
Cyprus.   The next port of call is Malta : an im-
pregnable island fortress, situated in the very
middle of the Mediterranean Sea.   Almost within
sight of this island, both to the north and south
of it, incessantly passes and repasses the stream of
shipping which carries the merchandise of the East
and the West.   Before we reach England we shall
once again stop : at Gibraltar, the key of the Mediterranean.   Many a time and stubbornly have
nations fought for the possession of it, but it is
England's now, has been for a century and more,
and seems likely so to remain.

I very much doubt whether this pre-eminence
of England is brought home to us quite vividly
enough.   We are rather too apt to look upon that
country merely as one among several great powers,
but we have far more to gain from her and to
learn from her, in industrial ways, than from any
other nation.   Our insular position and the quickness and aptitude of our population may one day
make us, as a maritime and commercial power, the
England of the East.

LETTER V.

MALTA, *September* 19*th*, 1888.

My last letter, written between Alexandria and Malta, went off to the post-office this morning the moment we arrived—just in time for the homeward mail. We are delayed here for a few hours by a slight accident to the machinery. I do not grudge the loss of time ; it will turn to gain in giving me a better opportunity of seeing the place, and will enable me to leave a few lines (which I shall finish when I get on board again) behind here to wait for next week's mail, not altogether without a faint-hearted wish that I were to accompany them, for I am divided between home-sickness and curiosity. On the one hand my friends, my books, my pleasant peaceful life, the familiar but ever beautiful landscape from my windows ; on the other my keen desire for this new world (which, by the way, they call the old world here) of which I have as yet seen so little and dreamed so much.

Later.—We shall not get away until midnight, or

perhaps even to-morrow morning, so I will make
the promised few lines into a respectable letter.

Malta is, if I may say so, at once ugly and
picturesque. Ugly because of the lack of vegeta-
tion and of the uniform baldness of a monotonously
undulating level, picturesque as it were by the
accident that the town and harbour form a pretty
picture—the harbours, I ought rather to say, for
there are two of them. These are separated by a
broad ridge, crowned with battlements and houses,
which is thrown out from the heights of the town
and slopes down to the sea in a north-easterly
direction. The main harbour spreads itself out
into a number of creeks, whose clear quiet waters
reflect the tall buttresses, houses and sea-walls
which spring up sheer from their depths. The
sunny air is merry with the sound of bells. There
are heavy, surly-looking armour-clads lying at their
buoys, a broad row of mercantile steamers with their
sterns tied to the wharf and their prows jutting out
into the harbour, a sprinkling of boats with white
awnings gleaming in the sun—very pretty, these
boats, graceful, with high-curved bow and stern,
though I do not think our light sampans yield to
them in point of looks. The English flag is over
all this: floats above the governor's palace, the
forts, the hospital ; flies at the ensign staff of the
ships, royal and mercantile—for the latter, too, are
nearly all English. English uniforms—soldiers' and
sailors'—are in the boats, in the streets, on the

dusty white roads outside the town.   The English
are red, clean, calm and silent ; the Maltese brown,
cool, clamorous and dirty.   The beggars are many
and importunate, some of them parading dreadful
diseases and hideous distorted limbs.

The island is little better than a flattish, arid
rock, cultivated with a patience and pertinacity
which would be admirable anywhere, but which
here fill up the measure of your admiration with
astonishment.   This bare rock—for the very fields
themselves appear to grow more stone than anything else—supports a population of some 150,000
souls, sober, industrious and docile.   It is said
the English are not liked by them, but they (the
Maltese) seem to live contentedly enough under
their rule.   For that matter, it must rarely happen
that a subject race *likes* its rulers ; it is well enough
when it does not cordially detest them.   Englishmen may not be individually very likable, but
they are at all events past masters in the art of
governing alien populations.   Their yoke is firm,
but their hand is light, for (and they do not forget
to remind the world of it) they are great respecters
of law and of individual liberty.   I was given to
understand (by an Englishman, it is true) that
what grumbling there may be against the masters
of the island mainly proceeds from the old Maltese
families of position, who are now naturally enough,
though not expressly, excluded from the exercise
of the political power once theirs.   But it appears

that the real grievance is a social one—the English higher classes pass for being very haughty and exclusive in their social relations with peoples under their rule.

I do not know that the Maltese have any more cause to grumble than has a man who is born poor, or weak, or blind, or foolish, or otherwise ill-affected. It is the fate of some individuals to be born slaves, in one sense or another; it is the fate of some populations to be in a state of relative political servitude. Were the Maltese never so brave and capable, they could not succeed in keeping Malta for themselves long. The island is too small, too poor to support, in addition to its working population, a garrison sufficient to protect it against a strong sea-power, to pay for guns, munitions of war, repair of fortifications, etc. Under modern conditions it is as certain as anything well can be, that Malta must always be under the dominion of some great power, and I do not suppose the inhabitants would gain much by changing masters. It is said the Italians are more akin to the Maltese than the English in language and temperament, and perhaps they would be personally more agreeable to them; but whether they would govern the people better is a question, while whether they would bring the inhabitants as much money and well-being is no question at all.

LETTER VI.

AT SEA, *September 22nd*, 1888.

A BRIGHT sunny day, hot, but tempered by a cool brisk breeze from the Gulf of Lyons to the north of us. Beneath the breeze and the sun the level waters sparkle and flash as only I have seen them at home in the inland sea. To the south-east, where the sun is, stretches out to the horizon an ever-broadening fan of light, set with brilliants of unimaginable lustre. As yet the sun has climbed but half-way up to the zenith, where the sky is of a dark blue, unfathomable. As he climbs higher and higher the blue will gradually fade up there, and give place to an increasingly intense white radiance. This, it seems, is an ideal Mediterranean day, and I can well believe it, for of its kind it is a perfect day. We are slipping easily and, but for the throb of the engine, noiselessly over a sapphire sea: dark blue sea below, dark blue sky above. Far away to the south, showing faint but delicately distinct through the clear air, run the high mountain ranges of North Africa, parallel with our course ;

28

they also have a faint tinge of blue resting on them
—a blue which verges on purple. Blue, the clear,
cold, pure colour, overspreads all things; purposely
put there, one might think, to rest the eye of man
from the glare and insupportable radiance of the
sun. Alas! European thought is a strong solvent
of our poetical but infantile beliefs. I remember
the time when, with a timid, faltering spirit, I
imagined I could trace here a line and there a
line in the vast design of creation, and would reach
out my hand through the gloom to seek the hem
of the Designer's robe. That time is past. I now
see nothing about and above me but a regular
succession of phenomena, which succession people
call by different names. The eagle can outstare
the sun, the owl can find his prey in the gloom;
man has to do a little of both, and man's eye has
been gradually adapted to the conditions of man's
life. . . .

The breakfast bell rang as I wrote down these
last words, which, now I re-read them, sound in
my ear as with the tinkle of argument. But I
have breakfasted, and am content now with the
lazy animal content of repletion. My thoughts
revolve with complacence about the more material
aspects of life, and that austerity which feeds on
the stomach's emptiness has disappeared to make
room for a more genial mood. You would not
agree, I know, with what I was about to set down.
I will not argue with you. I will forego the easy

advantage of putting my own arguments into your mouth and then proceeding to pulverise them at my leisure, as is the not infrequent custom with controversialists. Meanwhile, perhaps you would like to hear something about this life on board ship. I will cut very short what I have to say, for I am conscious that my presentment will appear even more desperately uninteresting than the reality.

The ship is full of English people, with a slight sprinkling of Germans and French. I have somewhere read a plausible argument that regularity and frequency of meals is an index of a high stage of civilisation. The wild man, the savage, eats irregularly, copiously, and at long intervals, for the simple and satisfactory reason that he often finds it difficult to procure food for himself, and makes the most of it when he does procure it. Settled habits of life, regularity of employment, etc., etc.,—you can guess all the argument without my setting forth. If it is at all true, it points to the English as having reached a high standard of civilisation, for they eat all the day long. My cabin steward calls me at half-past six or seven in the morning, and, before I am well awake, thrusts tea or coffee and biscuits under my nose. At nine o'clock there is breakfast, a very substantial meal. A little after midday comes another meal which is called "luncheon," just as substantial as the breakfast. Regularly, at about four o'clock in the afternoon, I notice a depletion of the numbers on the upper deck. At first I knew not what to make of this, but one day I had laid down my book about this time and was strolling on deck, when I happened to look down through the skylight into the saloon. To my astonishment they were all eating again,—a kind of unofficial meal this, consisting of cakes, bread, biscuits and tea. These trifles do not deter them from sitting down two or three hours later with excellent appetite to dinner, the amplest and most elaborate meal of the day. Englishmen have the reputation of great physical energy, and the latter perhaps accounts for their remarkable powers of eating,—or am I inverting cause and effect? So far as energy is in question there is a well-marked difference between the English passengers and the few others of distinct nationality who are to be found on board. The former are always on the move. They walk briskly up and down the deck. They play at games which require physical exertion. In the early morning I have seen the younger men whirling about heavy clubs and leaden weights, and fighting mock duels with padded hands—boxing, they call it. None of the other passengers do these things, but rather look on them with secret astonishment. Apparently, then, there is in English men a superabundance of physical energy, which requires daily dispersion. As a matter of fact we perceive that it does disperse itself in every corner of the globe.

On the whole, in fine weather, in a large vessel, and for a time, life at sea is not unpleasant, especially to a man of sedentary habits and contemplative cast of mind.   What it may be to those who make the sea and sea-faring their profession I know not. Sailors are proverbially grumblers, but they are cheerful withal and seem in general to be healthily constituted in mind and body.   They laugh readily and good-humouredly ; and when perchance something occurs to annoy them, they heartily and indiscriminately curse every one and every thing, and straightway forget their trouble.   Some of my fellow-passengers are evidently impatient of a long voyage ; you notice it by their inability to settle down to any occupation.   Some of them, again, not only bore themselves, but bore others.   A day or two after we left Nagasaki one of them lounged up and addressed me with : " Bound for England, sir ? "   " Yes," I answered.   " Ah ! you have a long journey before you.   Life on board ship, sir, is very monotonous.   Doctor Johnson, one of our classical authors, has remarked that a vessel is a prison with the additional chance of being drowned." He smiled a gratified smile, and turned away to address some one else.   I was about to make a note of this saying of Dr. Johnson, which struck me at the time as clever, when I heard my friend again, not far off : " As Dr. Johnson observes, a ship is . . ."   I then knew there was no need for

me to make that note. Between Nagasaki and
Aden I heard this excellent man remark on Dr.
Johnson's saying a great many times, and I cannot
say how often I espied that gentle smile of content
irradiate his features ; its appearance was periodical
and regular, like that of a revolving light on a
headland, alternately revealed and obscured.
Great is the power of words deftly put together !
This amiable person evidently believed he was
saying something which represented the state of
his own mind with regard to the sea and to ships,
as well as that of the Dr. Johnson aforesaid ; yet
throughout the voyage he has so far been con-
sistently cheerful and contented. People speak of
the monotony of a life at sea as if that decided the
question. But the truth is that monotony is not
inconsistent with contentment, or even with happiness ; indeed, every well-ordered life has an innate
tendency to what ill-regulated lives feel as monotony,—a sentiment which savours rather of age
and of experience than of turbulent youth ; but
the remark is yours, and I have treasured it for
wisdom's sake.

GIBRALTAR, *September 24th.*

There is no time to land and inspect Gibraltar.
We remain here only a couple of hours, so I must
be content to see what I can of the place from the
deck of the steamer. What I do see is a high
rocky hill connected with the mainland of Spain

by a narrow strip of sand some hundred *ken* in length.[1] The town, which with difficulty climbs a short way up the flank of the hill, looks uninteresting—as, indeed, does the whole place, to any one but a soldier or military engineer. I am told the face of the rock is pierced with masked batteries, but not a trace of them does the naked eye perceive. A hostile fleet would soon, doubtless to its own cost, discover their positions. It would be a fine sight, of the barbaric kind, to witness such an engagement. In imagination I see this splendid natural fortress wreathed with fire and smoke, I hear the thunders of its five hundred guns. The instinct of the savage is but half smothered in us,—with which pregnant and original remark I will bring my letter to a close. Adieu, dear and honoured friend! you will not again hear from me until I am settled in London.

---

[1] A *ken* is equal to about two yards.—ED.

LETTER VII.

LONDON, *October 4th*, 1888.

No fixed address as yet. Will you please continue to send your letters through our legation? . . . I have received from our friend Mr. X. an invitation to stay at his house, which I have accepted; it will give me a useful and interesting glimpse of the interior economy of an English household.

So soon after my arrival in London I am barely myself. My mental condition is invertebrate; I am too confused, too dazed as yet, to give you a clear outline of my impressions; as for the picture, finished in detail, you may have to wait long. I see many things at once, and nothing clearly.

Our steamer went right up the Thames to the eastern quarter of the metropolis, to the docks and wharves which for miles line the banks of the river, spreading thence inland into basins so crowded with shipping that one might imagine all the fleets of the world were laid up for repair in this one spot. Of the river and its immediate surroundings all that I recall has merged itself into a vast array of masts, funnels and rigging, which fades away into mere indistinctness as the train speeds towards the central part of the capital.

There is no town in Japan with which I could compare London so as to give you a fair notion of it. Pekin, in extent and population, is said not to fall far short of it. But a comparison of that kind only produces a false general impression, because it directs attention to points of similarity which are more or less accidental, and withdraws it from others which are essential. To compare London with Pekin is, as it were, to compare a vigorous active man with a decrepit recluse. Were I asked what is the dominant note in my mind concerning London, what is the impression which at once resumes and effaces the multitude of lesser ones, I would say : life, intense vitality both of mind and body; intensity and permanence of endeavour. No one who is accustomed to the semi-somnolence of most Oriental cities, excepting our own, can have any conception of this vast activity. There are hundreds (I am afraid to say thousands) of railway trains which leave London and enter it *daily*; there are tens of thousands of carriages (horse) which circulate in the streets, rapidly and noisily. The people themselves are all and always in a great hurry. They do not appear to understand the mere joy of existence apart from the business of life. There is no

pleasant appearance of repose and leisure about
them, consequently no look of dignity, either in
manner or carriage.   An all-pervading air of
anxiety, of preoccupation, of care, forms a striking
contrast with the stolidity of feature common to
the generality of Eastern populations, and one no
less striking with the gaiety and cheerfulness which
characterise our own.   The intellectual activity of
the capital is wonderful, to judge by the mere
outward signs of it.   In London alone there are
published about seven hundred different newspapers.   As for books, their number is as that of
the stars of heaven ; but people who pretend to
know aver that their light is not as of the stars.

Let it not annoy you if I throw off my observa-
tions in a bald and disjointed manner.   So much
of all this is new to me, and strange, that I find
myself as yet quite unable to co-ordinate my
thoughts, to marshal them into some sort of order
and coherence.   I scarcely know where to begin,
or how.   One thing at least I perceive, plainly
enough : little is to be known of a land or of a
people from its books ; or, at least, much less than
is generally thought.   A thousand details, familiar
to the writers of the books from infancy, and
equally familiar to those for whom they are written,
are omitted from the picture—the reader unconsciously supplies them from his own store of
observation.   For my part, I find I have steadily
and unconsciously filled up the English outlines

supplied to me with Japanese details, and am now looking in vain for the expected original.

Had I been writing these lines twenty years ago, or at least before the restoration,[1] it would have been an interesting matter to investigate how far the most striking contrasts between London and Kiôto or Tôkio are due, not to physical causes, such as differences of climate, materials of construction, etc., but to the dissimilarity in the social and political organisation of the two peoples. Constricted thoroughfares and narrow, high, parkless dwellings on the one hand ; broad streets (that is, comparatively to the amount of traffic), low roomy houses and spacious yashikis on the other : the former doubtless due to the land hunger which is bred in commercial centres of importance ; the latter an outward and visible sign of the feudal organisation of society—so far, at least, as the yashikis, with their vast enclosures and thousands of indwelling retainers, are concerned. With the putting-on of the forms of industrialism all this must suffer change ; the silent spaces of those park-enclosed residences will be invaded by the busy artisan and the profit-mongering shopkeeper, and our aristocracy will be gone (in fact, *is* gone) in all but name.

Earthquakes being practically unknown in this part of the world, the houses are built of brick and

---

[1] *I.e.*, of the Mikado, in 1868, to his ancient power and position.—ED.

stone.   In many parts of London these do not
represent any ideal of beauty with which I am
familiar, but rather a commercial or utilitarian
ideal, a typical expression of which may be found
in the rows of dry-goods boxes which we have often
enough seen discharged on the wharves of Yoko-
hama.   Take one of these boxes and squarely
punch some oblong holes in it to represent windows, and you will derive from the result of your
handiwork a tolerably good idea of the bulk of
London houses.   Where the rich dwell, however,
in the western quarter of the town, some of the
houses are not ill-looking, being decorated with
formal sculptured patterns, and with a sign of grace
in the occasional presence of leaf and flower in the
recesses of the windows.   Rich and poor alike
build their houses actually *on* the streets ; very few
dwellings are enclosed for the sake of privacy or
seclusion, as in our rich quarters.   Greed of any
space, however small, which may be utilised for
purposes of commerce is no doubt responsible for
this, as also for the manner in which the houses
grow to an astonishing height ; some of the newer
buildings ranging from six to twelve storeys !   Need-
less to say that private parks and gardens are very
rarely to be met with.   The eye is but seldom made
glad with trees and flowers, save in the public parks ;
even in these the lack of skill in horticulture and
of taste in grouping and training lead to disappointment.   The parks are many and large, but, like the

people, somewhat sad-looking and formal—rather health-insuring than pleasure-giving. Perhaps I am a little prejudiced. Beauty is no doubt relative to and tightly bound up with custom. In the course of time we shall perhaps become alive to the beauty with which industrialism clothes the matter on which it works, here through man's agency, there through nature's—from a dry-goods box to the formless canopy of fuliginous smoke which over-hangs London as I write.

LETTER VIII.

YASHIRI TO TOKIWARA.

TOKIO, *October 28th*, 1888.

PRAY make no apologies, my dear young friend, about what you write to me. Is it not part of our compact that you shall write what you think, with just the modest if unexpressed reservation that you shall think a little of what you write? And, surely, I can have no complaint to make on that score; indeed, I am not sure but that you think too much. Thus, about those dead firemen : I own I was but moderately impressed by that episode. It is true that things heard move us much less than things seen; but have I not seen in 1868, and again in 1877,[1] society, in the prosecution of its aims, slay its tens of thousands? Why so much pother over two dead firemen? Your friend the Englishman, who accepts the situation in a spirit of equanimity so truly philosophical, is in the right so far as his head is concerned; his heart, perhaps, is a little sluggish for want of training. I own that I am a little impatient of formal reasoning on such matters

---

[1] The latter date is that of the Satsuma rebellion.

41

—perhaps, as an old man, a little inaccessible to new ideas. Is not all that politico-economic talk rather wide of the mark—a helpless circling round the question, instead of going straight to the heart of it? And the heart of it is this : Will the ocean passengers and letter-writers suffer the delay of some hours in the voyage, or shall a certain number of firemen suffer death to prevent the delay? Obviously this is not a question which requires any very ingenious intellectual exercise for its solution.

The more your knowledge of men enlarges, the more plainly you will perceive that the world is very careless of suffering, especially of suffering which is borne in silence ; but not altogether careless, mark you, because so borne, for I will do it (the world) the justice of saying that it more often unconsciously overlooks suffering than con-sciously acquiesces in it. We are all in so great a hurry, there is always so much bustle about us, that we pay little attention to anything save what is imperiously thrust upon our notice.

Notwithstanding your covert irony, I well know that the modern utilitarian ideas which underlie the social economy of the western nations possess considerable attraction for you. You believe them to be based on an accurate knowledge of human nature, and therefore permanently applic-able. I believe them to be accurate so far as they go, but they do not go nearly far enough. On the other hand the dream of the idealist is like the fair image which decks with gracious but lying promise the dreary expanse of the Saharan desert—pleasant for the eye to rest on, but very disenchanting to the thoughtful mind thirsting for facts.

That much of men's traffic with one another is based on competition, friendly and unfriendly, is very true, but it is none the less so that one of the most imperative conditions of a man's happiness is to be found in that of those who immediately surround him. Now, the progress of civilisation, by which I understand the increasing of man's happiness, surely in a great measure consists in the growth of man's sympathy with his fellow-men, in his widening capacity to comprehend, and to associate himself with, their ways, their work, and their desires. Never perhaps was a truer or more significant thing said than that if you wish to understand any man or thing you must learn to love him or it. But the converse of this is true also; so that the expansion of the intellect and the increase of knowledge carry with them a greater power of love, a wider range of sympathy : a temper of affectionate admiration for the men and things which you recognise as great and worthy, of compassionate tenderness for those which appear to you as weak and trivial. But if it is indeed true that the progress of man and the advance of civilisation are marked by the growth of sympathy of man with men of all sorts and conditions (and the spread of the socialistic idea in Europe seems in relation to this to be evidence well worth pondering), if one of the causes of man's happiness lies in that of others, how foolish must those people be who set themselves and their followers to breast the stream of time, who preach, as a condition of social progress, the necessity and wisdom of leaving untrammelled the egotistic tendency of the individual—as if, forsooth, it were possible to live one's own life well without living well in the life of others.

The account of your short visit to Egypt interested me more than any other part of your two letters. I wish you could have told me more. The impression of melancholy, the feeling of sadness impressed upon you by the sight of those surprising memorials of the past, is one which I fully understand. It springs from the recognition of the sense of failure in human effort to realise that which it proposes to itself as an end. But the fault lies also to some extent in yourself. You are a little sluggish to the attraction of hope, which, after all, is the sure loadstar of a man's life. Discipline your imagination and your feelings : this is an old man's advice, one who loves you and would see you happy. Now let me tell you that those people of old Egypt toiled and moiled, thought and acted, fought and bled and suffered for other and far higher purposes than they were fully conscious of. You, a denizen of the East, child of a civilisation distinct in numberless ways from that of the West, merely see in those pathetic remains the history of a great failure. We, in Japan, owe nothing to the Egyptians. Our civilisation is of indigenous growth, save in that which we have borrowed, either directly or through the Coreans, from China—which indeed is to except a great deal. But the civilisation of the West is a much more complex matter ; its continuity and development is of far longer standing than ours. You must look at Egypt with Western eyes. The old Egyptians did their share of the world's work in the West, and that work lives on. The pyramid may crumble to dust, the tomb moulder, the walls of the secret subterranean chamber fall in, but the spirit which informed them lives on to this day, and with more abundant life than was at all possible in that dim and distant past. How strange to think, too, that those gigantic remains are yet there, as it were of set purpose, to tell us a story every other intended record of which must almost necessarily have perished ! Irony has ever been an attribute of Fate. Here, so far as we know, was an expenditure of time and toil unparalleled in the world's history : the toilers had *their* object in view, but Fate too had hers, and calmly appropriated their work for her own ends : truly we cannot but be grateful to her for this, assured though we may be that she will serve us in no way differently.

LETTER IX.

YASHIRI TO TOKIWARA.

TOKIO, *November* 11th, 1888.

I CONFESS to an occasional feeling of impatience with young Japan, with you clever young men of the present day. Much as I like you all and admire your cleverness, I cannot share your opinions : of convictions I will not speak, for you have none. But I am not impatient because I cannot agree with you. The events of the past five-and-twenty years have reft too wide and deep a chasm between the thoughts and ways of my generation and those of yours to render possible any close agreement between us in opinion and conviction. My complaint is that while your words and even your acts show in favour of ener- getic reform, modelled on the West, your minds are really neutral : in a state of neutral equilibrium. You are intellectually indifferent. As I have just said, you are possessed by no convictions. *You*, for instance, what have *you* gained from your keen examination of Western ideas ? (I note, by the way, that contact with Western *things* is occasionally

46

in the nature of a shock.)   You have secured for
yourself a kind of plastic spirit, which yields easily
to every impression, unrecalcitrant, without prejudice, but also without belief, which is the mainspring of human action.   Now, I postulate that, as
there are things good and bad for the human body,
so there are things good and bad for the human
mind—good and bad for the individual, either
under the one head or the other—and by bad I
mean prejudicial to his happiness, which is that
which the whole of his nature incessantly seeks.
Therefore I say, reasonably, and feeling myself
free from the too often unconscious dogmatism
of old age, that this too plastic spirit, this state of
mind—the more open the more undefended—is a
danger to the individual.   For you do not leave
your body thus defenceless against the chances
and changes of life ; on the contrary, to the best
of your ability you defend it against the bad and
expose it to the good.   I know what you will say :
that there is much doubt in your mind as to what
is good and bad for it, that your first object is to
rid your mind of prejudice.   Well, that is a very
laudable desire, but the matter is one of extreme
difficulty and of considerable danger.   It is next
to impossible for the individual to distinguish in
his own mind what is prejudice—which, so far as
it is reasoned, I will define as judgment resting on
false induction based upon experience—from what
is belief, which, again so far as it is reasoned, I will

define as judgment resting on true induction based upon experience. This in itself is a source of danger, not to speak of the traps which reason, too often giving but little heed to the danger flag of experience, is ever prone to fall into. The gradual sifting of the good from the bad is the work of many men and many centuries. What is the life of one man? asks a Western sage.

For an intelligent man of action there is no possible basis of action other than that supplied by the general experience of his fellows. Let him take his stand upon that. He has need to be distrustful of his powers of reasoning far more than of that experience, faulty as it too often is. But young Japan is not of this opinion. Young Japan is over-inquisitive, over-subtle, greatly taken up with the vain attempt to get to the bottom of things, not realising fully that most things have no bottom, but a semblance of one only, upon which, strangely enough, both we and they may quite securely and comfortably rest if we do but sincerely believe the semblance to be a reality.

I confess again, with what grace I can, that I am struck dumb with bewilderment, to which clings something of admiration, at the intellectual gyrations and subtleties of young Japan. The adroit gymnast has always been to me, from youth to age, a very interesting person. Even in these declining years I observe him not without emotion, and marvel at the training, the endurance, and the nerve which enable him to perform successfully his astonishing feats.   Occasionally my admiration perilously borders on envy, and I too feel as if I would like to dazzle the crowd—which, at such moments, I do not realise to be an idle and gaping crowd.   I reflect, however, that the adroit gymnast is after all rather a useless person, even when scarce, and that were many of us to become gymnasts this world would tend to become a very dull one, and in the end to grow quite insufferable for want of attention to the ordinary business which life demands.   Thus, in a measure, do I look upon young Japan, upon our clever young men.   These intellectual gymnastics are much too clever to be useful.   A very few young men thus trained would be amply sufficient for us ; they would have the merit—I do not rate it very high—of amusing us ; but the trouble is that they are too many, and if the people too readily swallow their loose ideas and clever phrases they will be found before long in the condition of one whose stomach is full of saki and very empty of rice.

I rarely hear a question discussed by our amateur reformers without a certain admiration of the deft way in which they circle round about it.   The conclusion appears to me ever the same : that there are a dozen or more answers to any question, that any of these may be right, that none of them may be right, that there is no right and wrong, that there is right and wrong, but only from an

individual point of view, etc., etc.   How wearisome
to find the world about one thus of a see-saw ! to
be bid see all things in a state of flux, unstable,
with no fixed point wherefrom to measure anything
whatsoever !   But, says young Japan, this is actually
the case, this is the way of the world,—what shall
it profit us to blink the facts ?   Ah, my dear young
friends, is it indeed the world which is of a see-
saw, or your conclusions as to the world ?   In
either case I am not surprised that your heads turn.
As for mine, I desire to keep it straight for the
short time during which I shall yet carry it above
ground ; and so, though I listen to you, I do not
heed you.   You on your side, I fear, will but
better my instruction.

LETTER X.

TOKIO, *November 25th*, 1888.

AMONG the young men of my acquaintance who
are at all given to thinking on grave subjects I
notice a certain languor, discouragement, and even
hopelessness, which appear to spring from a too
acute and ever-present perception of the iron circle
of necessity within which move all things, including
human effort and human will.   I do not kick
against the iron circle of necessity—that were
foolish; but to some extent I ignore it, because
I find that the too continuous contemplation of it
impairs my powers and deadens my will.   It ought
not to follow that, because we recognise that every
effect is the inevitable result of a number of causes,
and that we ourselves, our acts and volitions, are
also effects of pre-existing or present causes,—it
ought not to follow, I say, that we should forget
or ignore the fact that we, in our turn, are in like
manner causes.   And yet what ought not appears
in some measure to be; the persistent perception
of the natural process of evolution seems in some

51

natures to be accompanied by a silent rusting and
overlaying of the springs of action, a slow poisoning
of the well of life.   It is an old malady under a
new name : the old doctrine of fatalism, from the
attacks of which the Eastern world as a whole has
suffered so much, and from which we ourselves
have as yet been so singularly free.   There is a
strange attraction for the mind in these impossible
problems; such, again, as the old and well-worn
controversy about free will.   And yet how useless
is their discussion !   It is strange that among the
many acute minds who have wasted their time over
the free-will argument the conviction did not
sooner appear that the discussion was indeed a
waste of time so far as a solution of the problem
was concerned.   An evenly balanced mind must
necessarily be content to hold judgment in suspense
when two equally credible witnesses testify against
one another.   On the one side a direct perception
or, say, a simple sensation of freedom ; on the
other an intellectual perception of its impossibility.
We might feel disposed to believe the second were it
not that in giving the lie to the first it damages the
credit of that upon which it is itself built up; every
intellectual perception ultimately depending for its
validity on the truth of simple sensations.   The
very usual argument against free will—*i.e.* that there
is no free will because the will yields to the strongest
motive—is one of those not unusual arguments in
which the conclusion which should be derived

from the premiss, by mistake slips into the premiss itself.   For the argument resolves itself into an assertion : the will is not free because it follows the strongest motive, and the proof of this is that the strongest motive is that which the will follows. But in truth this argument, if it prove anything, proves rather too much, for it does away with will altogether.   Under this light, the word " will " merely defines the consciousness of the ego follow-ing a motive—an entirely new signification.   But what am I chattering about?   It seems I have hoisted sail to the idle wind of metaphysics, and am driving the gods only know where—a most foolish proceeding towards the inane, such that an old man, whose life has been of action rather than words, should feel ashamed of.   Let me come back to the point of my last letter, which is that if clever young Japan wishes for stable reform, you clever young Japanese should make up your minds somewhat more resolutely as to the meaning of stability ; but first let the rough breeze of common sense blow away from your minds the nebulous mists looking through which you now see the lines of demarcation between right and wrong, good and bad, beautiful and ugly, shift and waver to your endless confusion.   Draw the lines firmly for your-selves.   Every such line must be arbitrary ; but, once drawn, your field will be free for action and your minds from nerveless hesitancy.

Your last letter, the first written from London,

has just arrived. It is pleasant to know that you
have reached your journey's end safely. I shall
now look forward to your letters with even increased
interest. Up to the present I have been travelling
with you, in recollection, over ground not unfamiliar to me; for although my visit to Europe of
fifteen years ago was very hurried because of the
pressing nature of the mission with which I was
entrusted, and which claimed all my time and
attention, yet I failed not to seize the few opportunities I had of getting a glimpse of things on my
way out and home.

Your first impressions of London are not unlike
those of other of our countrymen who have had
leisure or orders to go West. " Life," you say,
" intense vitality both of mind and body ; intensity
of permanence and endeavour ; " this sums up your
impressions. Most men rest on their impressions
without much thought, until use either stereotypes
or effaces them. But I know that will not be the
case with you. You will dwell on yours and draw
profit from them before they either disappear or
become part of you. Let me beg of you then,
presently, when you shall find yourself sufficiently
full of the *facts* of Western life, to pause and
consider : to what end strives this intensity, this
permanence of endeavour ? to what ideal of life
are these Western people thus responsive ? what is
the mainspring at the back of this clockwork ?—
the answer to which question is of the first import-

ance for us. I have my suspicion, my private opinion, I may almost say my conviction, as to what that answer may be, but will keep it to myself for the present. Meanwhile young Japan no doubt perceives plainly enough that these people are in earnest, are energetically in pursuit of something. The energy, indeed, is greatly to be commended, but it would be pleasant to feel more confidence about the application of it. It is just possible that young Japan's eyes are dazzled and delighted with the energetic blowing of soap-bubbles, iridescent, beautiful, yet, sad to think, filled with mere rank breath.

I return for a moment to my young friends who are given to thinking. Please do not imagine that I confound these with the kind of reckless, empty-headed reformers who are responsible for our recent student riots and other disorders of like kind. Mere mischief-makers, whether of the designing or feather-headed sort, will, I trust, be held in check by the firm hand of authority and the good sense of the people. But those who think to-day rule to-morrow. The thinkers of one generation mould the next. I do not look forward to the day of the coming generation with very sanguine feelings. Our clever, thinking young men are too exaggeratedly agnostic. With the best of these such disposition of mind leads to a mournful pessimism. But the soul cannot rest therein, flies therefrom, seeking relief from dull despondency.

From " all is vanity " the step is easy, well-nigh inevitable, to " let us enjoy to-day, for to-morrow we are not." An evil day it is for the nation whose leaders are thus minded. A French writer whom I have been reading recently says of his countrymen that there are among them too many ' qu'est-ce que cela me fait*istes* " and " cela m'est égal*iens*." These and, generally, those whose philosophy is summed up in " après moi, le deluge " are the fruits of exaggerated agnosticism, and the seeds of this fruit in their turn bring forth immorality in the nation and dishonesty in government.

CHAPTER XI.

TOKIWARA TO YASHIRI.

LONDON, *November* 28*th*, 1888.

I MAKE no apology for restricting myself, in my last two letters,[1] to matters of purely personal interest ; for, as to much which I saw around me, I felt the need of silence and self-concentration. To keep my eyes open and my mouth shut was, I knew, the only means of bringing order to the confused mass of novel impressions borne in upon me. I have in this met with but incomplete success, but between you and me there is no need of flourish and curvet—you will excuse any awkwardness in the manner of my task, provided the matter be forthcoming.

Considering the object I have in view, nothing appears to me to merit more attention than the origin and effects of what is termed, in this and other European lands, the middle class of society ; a class to which our own country cannot furnish any proper counterpart, for it is essentially a product of the industrial stage. The word " middle "

[1] Not supplied to the Editor.

57

is descriptive, for the class is such as you might imagine to stand between our working people on the one hand and the aristocracy and official class on the other, now that the cramping bonds of the feudal system have been removed. Picture to yourself the foreign colony in the treaty ports multiplied and dispersed all over the country, and you will form for yourself a notion of the kind of people who constitute a middle class. But I am disinclined, from lack of sufficient observation, to say more just at present about this matter. It is, as I think, one of the most important for us to comprehend. I will take yet a little time, and, later, the helping hand of opportunity.

Meanwhile, speaking of classes, nothing strikes me more than the difference in look and bearing between the upper and lower orders of society. In general, an Englishman of birth and breeding is tall and shapely of make, but the close-fitting garments are trying to any but a fine figure. An air of health, neatness and cleanliness of person pervades him. He is stiff, yet not awkward ; indeed, the stiffness is more apparent than real. The lower-class individual, on the other hand, is an inarticulate expression of all that is ungraceful, ungainly and slovenly. The outline of the figure is coarse and clumsy, though muscular. Vestments sit ill at ease on heavy, round-shouldered and often ignoble forms. As for the women (of the lower class) they invariably have a draggled-tail, unkempt appearance, rendered the more noticeable because throughout the feminine social hierarchy each class apes the dress and carriage of that above it, instead of selecting some apparel neatly adapted to whatever business or occupation necessity may impose. In address, the upper classes are polite and courteous, free from false emphasis, exaggeration and assumed servility of manner. The lower classes, on the contrary, are surly and unamiable; their bearing has about it a curious cross flavour of meanness and independence—the result, as it were, of the dull and degrading tasks of modern industry coupled with the exercise of political power. In every way the contrast between the upper and lower classes is so marked that I ask myself whether it is possible that the finer the flower of civilisation the more rank the soil in which it strikes root?

The sartorial art is, of all arts in London, that which best repays attention. The dress of an Englishman of fashion is by no means ill-imagined as a means to set off a fine figure. You must not judge of it by the Englishmen in our treaty ports, who wear clothes in order that they may be covered, whereas the London man of fashion wears clothes in order that he may be discovered. To be kept warm, to feel quite at ease, free to move his limbs easily, naturally and gracefully (if grace be in him), are not the objects first in importance with the man of fashion, but rather to be apparelled in accordance with the latest decisions of the leading tailors. The figure of a man is looked upon exclusively from a tailor's point of view—that is, as a form on which to exercise the utmost ingenuity and closeness of fit. The body is sheathed in a tight-fitting coat which reveals and, where desirable for beauty's sake, accentuates with deft art every curve of the outline. The neck is cased up to the chin in a linen strap (the collar) of the length and stiffness requisite in order that the head may be carried with due statuesque immobility. The fashion of tight garments prevails also with the women, and is carried by the fashionable of both sexes to excess. The arms, instead of hanging down the sides of the body easily and loosely, are turned with the elbows slightly outward, and, from shoulder to elbow, stand out at a perceptible angle from the perpendicular: to bring the elbows close to the side would be to risk bursting the seams of the garment. It must be owned that this style of costume is not becoming to every one. A short, corpulent, rotund man, for instance, with arms hanging out well away from the body, is not very unlike a perambulating inflated pigskin.

All this, however, is a mere matter of fashion in the metropolis—a fashion which is more idle than foolish, more foolish than hurtful—for Englishmen are essentially men who love action, if also parade. And when the time for action comes, the stiff costume of fashion is thrown aside for this or that other, always well fitted and appropriate to the occasion. Their fondness and aptitude for field sports, athletics, and many-sided adventure develop a fine form and a manly bearing. If they take pride in showing these off—pride which shows them not always to advantage—they take yet more in the skill and endurance which only physical exertion and resolute self-subjection to bodily hardship can permanently maintain.

The apparel of the women I will not enter into; it would no doubt be full of surprise even in speculative investigation, and is certainly too full in outward detail for my powers of description. There is one point, however, already often enough commented on at home, which nevertheless challenges observation again, in that it leads, oddly enough, to a comparison of the European æsthetic sense with that of the West African negro. I have recently read in an interesting and, I believe, veracious book of travels that the negro admires in his womankind a generous amplitude of posterior development. The same or a similar appreciation of this point of beauty is current in England and, so I understand, in Europe generally. But nature, so bountiful in many ways to our European brethren, appears in this respect to have been unkind, niggardly even. So, at least, I am bound to believe, for I gather that art has successfully stepped in to fill full the shortcoming of nature.

The subject of clothes leads me back naturally to that of tailors. I may notice, in passing, that there are points of similarity between tailors and Jews. The Jews (who, as you know, put to an ignominious death the founder of the Christian religion, and were therefore long regarded as the natural enemies of all Christians) have gradually emerged from a position of social and political degradation to one of absolute equality with the Christians, in England at least. The growth of tolerance, and especially the spread of all those ideas which are associated with industry and commerce, have brought this about. They have also brought about the emancipation of tailors from the bond of more or less good-natured popular contempt in which they have almost everywhere been held. It had at one time become a saying in England that it takes seven (or nine, I forget which) tailors to make a man. There is a story that the great Queen Elizabeth, in the sixteenth century, once greeted a deputation of fourteen (or eighteen) tailors with the finely humorous exclamation: "Good-day, gentlemen both!" Since those days the position and estimation of tailors have greatly changed, but with a difference, here, as compared to those of the Jews; for a Jew is still emphatically a Jew—as a rule he is proud of being so, and calls himself by a name which betrays his origin. But tailors, with that fine sense for form which their occupation might reasonably be expected to develop, now frequently call themselves, not tailors, but "artists in draping the human form." These artists, indeed, must be reckoned as a great force in the development of human affairs. In Europe dress exercises an influence which, considering its apparent soberness, is very remarkable to an Oriental. Many a young man's future turns less on his intrinsic qualities than on external graces of manner and dress. Many a worn-out voluptuary owes his few remaining successes to the perfect workmanship of sartorial artists. It may be said, indeed, that there is a sense in which may yet be applied the old saying that it takes seven (or nine) tailors to make a man.

LETTER XII.

TOKIO, *December 9th*, 1888.

IN my young days the best men wished to reform Japan, but they were content to let the rest of the world alone and to try to reform Japan on Japanese lines. The rest of the world was to them an indifferent matter. No doubt, in this they were at fault, but it seems easy to run into the opposite extreme. I, too, with no claim to be of the best, ardently desired to see changes effected and abuses removed. But the manner in which we set about these things was less admirable than the desire which spurred us to attempt them : the end sought was good, but the means employed were indifferent. This is the usual fate of reformers, who seem scarcely ever sufficiently alive to the fact that it is already a pretty hard task for any man to reform himself, let alone others. The truth is that the world is too full of reformers. Imagine how well the world might go were every reformer to cease trying to reform others and were to devote his attention to the reform of the person with whom

64

he is most intimately connected, leaving others to do likewise ! It is perhaps the feebleness, the pessimism, the lack of enthusiasm natural to old age, which suggest such thoughts to me ; but, allowance made for these inevitable defects, I still think that this way of reform would present many advantages over the usual one. Others before and far above me have thought so too, and have made not a little stir in the world, but their lessons are at present in disfavour, or out of fashion.

I would say to you all : make up your minds to believe in something ; you will then frame for yourselves an ideal to strive for, and you will be the happier for the striving. There is no greater mistake made than to suppose that a man cannot believe what he chooses ; indeed, he cannot choose but to believe if only he will set to work about it in the right way. A belief well chosen, whether by himself or by others for him, is an important element of happiness in a man's life,—and what does man seek if not happiness ?

But how, in the right way, to set about reaching a comforting and comfortable belief? I can tell you. You will recognise those who possess such belief by their serenity of soul and cheerful optimism under what others call the strokes of ill luck or misfortune. Nothing comes amiss to them. They are convinced that whatever happens to them is either for their immediate or ultimate good : a flawless armour this to their happiness. They

5

clearly discern God's finger tracing for them the
path which they are to follow ; and they follow it,
nothing doubting. Idealists, you will say. What
of that, if idealism leads to happiness ? I say,
then, seek out these men, make them your habitual
companions, submit your mind to the influence of
theirs, as you would submit your body to your
trusted physician ; try hard to look through their
eyes, to reason with their reason, however faulty
it may appear to you. Have they not found the
great secret ? In fine, take the advice tendered to
unbelievers by a great French writer, mathema-
tician and man of God ; a follower of Christ :—
" Suivez la manière par où ils ont commencé (that
is, the believers) ; c'est en faisant tout comme
s'ils croyoient, en prenant de l'eau bénite, en faisant
dire des messes, etc. Naturellement même cela
vous fera croire et vous abêtira." This is a piece
of advice which it is well worth while for any one
to ponder, and to ponder carefully—peculiarly
adapted, I rather think, to our clever reformers,
who are decidedly too clever : their wisdom would
wear better for some slight admixture of mere
sound instinct. It is far from my thoughts to
recommend the above-given advice as it stands :
somewhat too crudely put even for those to whom
it was particularly addressed. We possess a religion of our own. Let us cleave to that, steering
a parallel course to that indicated by the above-
quoted thinker. Yet, if this may not be, I would

rather see my countrymen Christians than pagans
or unbelievers. For all of us, Buddhists, Maho-
metans, Christians, etc., sail along parallel circles;
small circles, indeed, whose planes pass far from
the centre of the sphere of all things,[1] yet into
known ports of call and harbours of refuge lying
along them. But the unbeliever yaws ever at his
own pleasure, or follows the wind's; a pleasant
enough proceeding at times, especially in fine
weather, but which leads eventually into dangerous
waters, whence none but the hardiest and most
skilful escapes. Neither will it be the unbeliever
who shall strike into the great circle and pilot
humanity thereon. That day, however, and the
hero of it, are yet far distant. When mechanical
science shall have become the handmaiden of the
philosopher rather than of the merchant, when the
wisdom of the nations shall have been welded into
one, the nations themselves into a single family,
and a veritable son of man or leader of humanity
born of it, we shall be—drawing near the end of
things here. Meanwhile, in so distracted a time as
the present, any reconciler of disparate things shall
be welcome to us. After so much dismemberment,
pulling apart, analysis, dissection, we are but little

---

[1] The writer does not, I think, derive his metaphor from
Buddhistic philosophy, but rather from the art of navigation :
a " great circle " is one the plane of which passes through the
centre of the sphere ; small circles are parallel to a great circle,
and, consequently, do not pass through the centre.—ED.

advanced : the same materials as of old lie before
us, obstinate, unyielding, only to be put together
again in much the same form : organic growths,
rather, with self-shaping power, not plastic material
to be shaped at alien will.   Could we but leave off
tinkering for a little, and watch the form and
growth-tendency of the plants whence we have
derived our grafts, it would be well.   We are
known for skilled horticulturists, and, as such, admired.   But, though genuine the admiration, it is
tinged with contemptuous wonder at the grotesque
abortions which it pleases our clever gardeners to
produce.

LETTER XIII.

TOKIWARA TO YASHIRI.

LONDON, *December* 12*th*, 1888.

ON many minor matters my notions of things European have been much modified since my arrival, even in such things as I might reasonably have expected to learn from books. For instance, I seemed clearly to have understood that a constitutional sovereign was one who governed according to the constitution or body of the law and customs of his country; but, judging by what I see and hear in England, the model constitutional country, this is certainly not the case. It can scarcely be said that the Queen of England governs according to the constitution, unless we please to be paradoxical and add that, according to the constitution, the Queen does not govern. Most European sovereigns are constitutional, more or less; but the less any one of them has to do with the constitution the more constitutional he is. Thus, in England, where the share of power allotted to the throne in matters of government is almost nominal, the sovereign is truly constitutional. The Queen's subjects, or that portion of them which forms the electorate, possess the substance of power; she, the shadow and the name of it. It would not be altogether absurd to compare her position with that of the Mikado before the restoration, her ministers and people standing to her in much the same relation as did the Shôgun and his feudatories to the Mikado. The Queen, like the Mikado, is the head of the national church, but her person is not held in the same awe and reverence as was, and still is, that of our own sovereign. In this, as in many other matters, the English show their indifference to precision and congruity of ideas and their leaning to compromise and common sense: the sense, that is, which is common to the great mass of fairly educated and intelligent persons; the sense which is cautious and methodical, careless of symmetry between theory and practice, impatient of logic, wanting in subtlety and accuracy of distinction. There is much praise of common sense in England, but it is not always very well bestowed. What the English people most surely and promptly recognise is that the common-sense view of any matter is that which must inevitably be submitted to. It is this common sense, indeed, which, always and painfully following in the wake of the more trained intellects, rules the world. Everything, be it good or bad, which is set up in direct opposition to it, suffers destruction, or, in the rare instances when this is not the case, common sense is thrown into confusion, and anarchy follows. In more ways than one this general sense is analogous to the common instinct of the lower animals. Imagine a clever ant who should submit to his tribe plans for the removal of a stone or other obstacle from one of the main thoroughfares of the ant community. I see the bewilderment, the alarm, the hurried confusion of the tribe; I hear the outcry, the opposition. The fact is that the ants regard this stone not as an obstacle, but as a landmark without which they imagine they could not get on; they would sooner have the trouble of climbing over it than miss it from their path; and had the clever ant been just a little more clever, he would have known that the work of imagination is more irremovable than stones or even mountains, and he would wisely have kept his plans to himself.

The sovereign of this country is called "The Supreme Head on Earth of the Church of England." This is a fine title, though it seems a little complicated and smacks somewhat of compromise. It lacks the simplicity and nobleness of our Tenshi.[1] Moreover, with us the name and the thing are closely correlated; the name stands for something real in the eyes of the people, and so stood even during the long temporal eclipse of the true sovereign.[2] The Mikado, acknowledged in heart

---

[1] " Son of Heaven."

[2] By the beginning of the seventeenth century the temporal power of the Mikado had entirely passed out of his hands into those of the Shôgun and his feudatories.

belief, as well as by the more or less idle wagging
of tongues, as the descendant and representative of
the gods, is invested by the people with more than
human dignity and sanctity.   In old Japan he was,
in young Japan he still is, the true head of the
national church.   The English sovereign, on the
other hand, in religion as in politics, is merely an
august figure-head.   The Supreme Head of the
Church (who, it would seem, should in a manner
be the Vicar of God) has absolutely no power worth
mentioning, either spiritual or temporal, over the
Church.   And where do you suppose resides the
power, both temporal and spiritual?—In parliament.
Parliament has prescribed what the people shall
believe, or, to put it a little less strongly, it has
settled what the priests or bonzes shall teach and
how they shall conduct their ceremonial.   The
prime minister, who is responsible to parliament,
appoints the bishops and archbishops (chief bonzes).
With this eminently practical people the question
is mainly one of work to be done and payment of
wages to those who do it.   The people, directly or
circuitously, pay the priests, and the people therefore
decide, through their representatives, what manner
of work the priests shall do, what the priests shall
be directed to teach them.   On the whole then, the
doctrine taught tends to become a comfortable one.
The disagreeable future penalties attached to present
ill-conduct and hardness of belief—such as roasting
at hell fire and being put to various horrible tortures

for eternity—are being gradually relegated to a dim, distant and shadowy background. It is noticeable that in the Roman Catholic Church these pains and penalties are yet kept well in the forefront of doctrine; the fact is significant, because the Roman Catholic Church, wherever established in those Western lands, occupies a more independent and dignified position than do the Reformed Churches, it lies less at the mercy both of popular whim and of independent thought, it preserves unchanged the even tenor, the steady persistency of its way. It is not difficult, even for a foreigner, to perceive that in the Reformed Churches of Europe there is an element of change, a canker of dissolution which will probably prove fatal to them. At all events, seeing what the government and organisation of the Christian Church is in England, the less we say at home about its spiritual independence the better it will be for our candour and the more creditable to our understanding. It is true, however, that many thinking men here make a distinction between the Christian religion and the religion of Christ.

Tokio, *December 23rd*, 1888.

LAST week I made acquaintance with an Englishman who has come here with the object of seeing for himself something of our land and people. He is a member of the English House of Commons, and belongs to the advanced party in politics. I do not precisely know in which direction this party desires to advance, nor do I greatly care ; but, if I may judge from one or two individuals, I should say that, like our own advanced party, though perhaps in a yet higher degree, it lacks advancement in the acquiring of that gentle tact and good breeding which not only makes social intercourse a pleasant pastime, but which, in the propaganda of ideas and of programmes of action, is more valuable even than sound argument. But perhaps I do my own people a wrong by comparing them with foreigners in this respect. Most of the foreigners whom I have met are deficient in the polite amenities, and this gentleman was no exception to the general rule. Thus, he must have perceived very plainly, from the general tenor of my conversation, that neither in matters relating to the state nor in those relating to society am I an advocate of new things taking the place of old ; yet he was at no pains to hide from me that in his estimation those who stand athwart the path of so-called reform are merely stupid or obstinate or self-interested persons. Half vexed and half amused, I listened to his bubbling prattle of progress, to the easy volubility with which he applied, to Eastern conditions and Eastern problems, ideas and propositions originating in the entirely different conditions and problems of the West. He professed—not without a veiled tone of condescension—much delight with us for the celerity with which we have put on (aped, I call it) the forms of European civilisation. His astonishment was unfeigned when I expressed my sense of shame and ridicule at all this ignoble posturing and grimacing in borrowed clothes, this apish or, at best, infantile trick of imitation, which will before long earn for us among our neighbours a title to be known as "the performing dogs of the East."

In connection with our clownish adaptations of the garb and ways of Europe, which formed the staple of our conversation, there were as usual the infallible congratulations on the abandonment of what they and too many of us are pleased to name the barbarous customs of the duel and the *harakiri*. Of the duel I will not now speak ; there is perhaps

as much to be said against it as for it, and never
at any time have I been a fanatical upholder of it.
But of the *harakiri*—that consummating act by
which a brave man quits a life which has become
insupportable to his honour—it were traitorous to
my best instincts to say aught against it.   If a man
is deserving of or has to suffer death, it is surely
more decorous and more manly that he should
inflict the penalty with his own hand than that he
should—like a sheep or an ox—be led to the
shambles and despatched by that of the executioner.
Our well-intentioned reformers, both foreign and
indigenous, condemn *harakiri* without well understanding what it is which they condemn.   They
fail to draw a clear distinction in their minds
between the method of punishment and the authority by which it is, or was, adjudged and imposed.
It was really the latter with which they were dissatisfied, not altogether without reason.   Perhaps
I do not make my meaning quite clear.   What I
wish to convey is that I fully recognise what force
there is in the objections urged against the old
régime, under which the power of life and death
was vested in one man, whose expression of displeasure was equivalent to a sentence of death.
But I do not perceive how this tells against the
mode of punishment.   I do not understand why
the old and time-honoured custom of the *harakiri*
should not co-exist with the establishment of the
Western forms of criminal justice.   Be the form of

trial what you will, and who you will the authority adjudging the sentence, neither the one nor the other affords a good reason for abolishing *harakiri*. On the contrary, the democratic notions 'which are afloat just now in men's minds, inclining them to efface distinctions of caste and class, encouraging them (if we are to entertain the advanced views) to look to personal honour rather than to social position as the best claim to popular esteem, should be used as ready levers for re-establishing in popular reverence this old and honourable custom; to the extent, at all events, of recommending it and eventually enforcing it by sheer strength of public opinion in all cases where death becomes by law imperative to any man, be he of high degree or low in the social scale. The cowardly wretch whose heart fails of courage, and arm of strength, to inflict the blow, should be led to the slaughter-house with marks of disgrace, but the seal of popular approbation should be set on him who knows how to die bravely, even though disapprobation load his memory for not having learnt to live well.

The fact is that your European friends are infected with prejudice in this matter of the *harakiri*, and they have carried the infection into our midst. Those among us who condemn the custom have been led to do so by an ape-like propensity to imitation; they have never paused to consider that the nations of the West, albeit more mobile

and energetic than our neighbours, are no more
than these free from prejudices. The hostility of
the European peoples, and of their offshoots in
other parts of the world to any form of suicide, in
whatever circumstances and from whatever motive
prompted, is founded not on the broad common
sense of mankind, but on religious bigotry. Tried
by the opinion and practice of the great races and
nations of the world, both in the past and in
the present, this hostility stands condemned as
unreasonable and unreasoning.

LETTER XV.

LONDON, *December* 26th, 1888.

THE upheavals, revolutions and internecine struggles which mark the history of the social development of Europe have made it impossible for any one family in any one country of this part of the globe to retain possession of a throne for more than a few hundred years. Nowhere in Europe is it possible to find a parallel to our unbroken succession of sovereigns from the remotest historical times to the present day. In point of family all the European sovereigns are mere plebeians when compared with ours. They all are, and long have been, the vulgar persons which ours are on the eve of becoming. They move about in public, are seen of their subjects, eat with them, drink with them, on occasion even jest with them. Familiarity breeds contempt, as they say here; and truly they have every right to say so who dismiss sovereigns as you or I might dismiss a lacquey who had incurred his master's displeasure.

The most real power of the sovereign here appears to lie in the influence which he or she exerts over the manners and morals of the upper class of society. This class in some measure takes its tone from that of the court, and the tone of the court during the reign of the present sovereign is considered to have been excellent. To judge of the morality of a people is always a hard matter for a stranger. The question presents itself, in fact, whether it is possible to consider a nation as either moral or immoral, seeing that codes of conduct differ one from the other, and that each nation has its own code, which has grown with it and become part of it. From this point of view it may of course be urged that a moral people is one which closely cleaves to a narrow routine of habit and to a rigid rule of convention, those individuals which depart therefrom—the immoral ones—being few in number compared with the mass. But it appears scarcely possible to establish a comparison between nations on this basis. There is, however, a kind of immorality which it seems to me may be imputed to a whole people. It is that species of hypocrisy in virtue of which certain derogations from habit and convention are secretly submitted to while openly reprobated, or, where it is possible to do so, ignored as if they were non-existent. Often enough such derogations are merely the birth of new customs or conventions, but, morality being conceived as fixed and unalterable, it follows that the changes, though perhaps necessary, are looked upon as immoral until they become firmly established. The rather prevalent opinion that this kind of hypocrisy is largely practised in England is not, I think, well-founded. This nation, taken as a whole, attaches immense importance to what in its sincere but often purblind view it regards as right or moral conduct. There is in England very little of the delightful *insouciance* of our French friends—of the gentle shrug of shoulder when matters of public or private morality are in discussion. The great bulk of the people look at such matters with great seriousness, and are inclined to be shocked if you venture to speak of them in the spirit of *persiflage.* Some nations are priest-ridden, others mob-ridden, all more or less fool-ridden. In England the moralist is in the saddle (their greatest art-critic, Ruskin, is a moralist in disguise), and thus a tendency is established to set up, and compel homage to, a standard of morality to which a very great number of persons cannot possibly attain. As a consequence of this, there is bred in immoral individuals a strong desire to conform in appearance with the recognised standard ; and this leads, in very many cases, to an affectation or simulation of morality which in some countries, ours included, would be felt by all to be distasteful, more repulsive indeed than immorality itself.

This kind of hypocrisy exists, of course, in

6

every country, but the stranger in England is apt
to over-estimate it by confounding with it mere
squeamishness. Thus the great mass of Englishmen of the upper and middle classes show an
anxious care for the innocence and purity of their
womankind. Whenever in England any of the
impurities of social life rise to the surface so as to
be plainly seen of all men, there is an effort, on the
part of the more reputable portion of society, to
cover them up, to push them down again, to get
them out of sight in one way or another, partly
from a sense of shame that such things should be,
partly from a desire that the innocent and virtuous
should not be exposed to the risk of contamina-
tion. Hundreds of thousands of good women are
brought up in entire ignorance of the existence of
many of the so-called social evils, and live their
life through in ignorance and purity. This system
of education, preserving as it undoubtedly does a
sprinkling of individuals in spotless purity of mind
and perfect propriety of conduct, tends to preserve
and foster purity and propriety in the mass of the
people, but surely in a very inefficient manner ; for
this kind of virtue can possess but very little
strength or backbone, being necessarily deficient
in the skill and endurance which exposure to and
victory over evil can alone build up. Doubtless,
by taking pains and precautions, by practising a
system of strict isolation, you may succeed in preserving some proportion of a population from the

terrible contagion of small-pox; but, take it all round, the safest mode of diminishing the hold of the malady on the people will be to subject the entire population to the milder contagion of the vaccine lymph.

I return, as I promised to do in a former letter, to the subject of the middle class of society in Europe. The essential feature of a middle class lies in its being distributive. By this I mean that most of the persons who compose it are engaged in the labour of distributing the produce of agriculture and industry: the labour of turning into the numberless streams, streamlets and rills of supply the various productions of the country itself and of foreign countries, whether as great merchants or as small traders and shopkeepers. The term " middle class " is elastic. It certainly includes more than the distributive class proper: it includes, for instance, at least in name, the great manufacturers and employers of labour; at least in name, I say, for these persons, what with their wealth and influence, may now be regarded as forming part rather of the upper than of the middle class. This is natural enough in a country whose boast it is that its position among the nations rests mainly upon its industrial supremacy.

It was the slow up-growth and expansive force of the middle classes which, in Europe, burst the bonds of the feudal system; and the growth of the middle class was due, inevitably, to the development of commerce, both national and international. International trade, initiated by the Western spirit of enterprise, fostered through the political sagacity of Western princes (who perceived, in the spread of industrialism and the growing wealth and power of industrial centres, the readiest and surest method of overcoming the power and quelling the turbulence of their feudatories), was the prime cause of the gradual revolution of European mediæval society. Industrial development went hand in hand with extension of international commerce, each at once the cause and the effect of the other, in accordance with the law of interaction which is everywhere noticeable in the affairs of men. At the present time, the greater the trade of a country, especially its foreign trade—an index of superabundant energy and enterprise—the more numerous and influential the middle class. As an instance of this, compare England with Russia. The total annual value of the foreign trade of the United Kingdom is computed to be now about six hundred millions sterling, —that of Russia about one hundred millions. In England the middle class is numerous, wealthy and politically powerful; in Russia it is quite otherwise. In England, until quite recently— before the extension of the franchise—the middle class was the final arbiter in all political matters of moment; in Russia, the middle class, as a power in politics, is practically non-existent.

LETTER XVI.

YASHIRI TO TOKIWARA.

Tokio, *January 7th,* 1889.

THE English newspapers, which I regularly look through, give us on occasion the benefit of their advice and encouragement, for which we are very thankful. They pat us on the back in the half admiring, half condescending manner which is peculiar to the English. When I observe an intelligent performing dog, my feelings are probably an index of those with which the average Englishman observes us : the condescension is towards the dog, the admiration is of myself, because of the condescension. The newspapers of other nations do not appear to trouble themselves greatly about our proceedings, or even our existence, so that I imagine it has by informal but common consent been left to the English to supply the current criticism of the events of the day throughout the habitable globe. Especially does this appear to be with the representative of the ordinary educated English idea : *The Times. The Times* approves, disapproves, smiles, frowns ; now sternly shakes its

85

august head in solemn reproof, now gently wags it in sapient commendation, thus discharging the office of censor for the benefit of the nations at large. We, among the nations, thus occasionally get the opportunity of more closely watching that our feet do not stray from the path of wisdom; and for such opportunity we are, as I have already said, and honestly, very thankful—albeit thankfulness may occasionally show an irritable fringe of impatience. It is, in truth, as impossible not to admire, as not to be occasionally provoked by, *The Times*. The extent, variety and sureness of its information are surprising, the vigorous common sense of its staff of writers is soothing and reassuring. You feel, when you read *The Times*, that you are safe from the delusive brilliancy of mere cleverness or the aberrant strokes of genius; it is all solid, satisfying and withal satisfactory. And yet your vigorous and victorious common sense is a dreadful begetter of dogmatism precisely in those matters which lie beyond its accustomed ken. Thus, although I cannot but feel grateful to *The Times* for the genuine good feeling which it displays towards us and the good opinion it entertains of us and of our capabilities, yet am I impatient of the too persistent manner in which our hasty footsteps are belauded, and our much-suffering feet encouraged along the road of Western civilisation. Because, in the course of five-and-twenty or thirty years, we have succeeded without serious harm or convulsion in presenting to an astonished world a counterfeit likeness of European ways, it is assumed that what we have done has been wisely done. These Western people do not suspect that much of the web of change, which we have so rapidly and dexterously spun about ourselves, may be and probably is far more a result of the extraordinary versatility and love of imitation characteristic of the nation than of any radical necessity, tendency or desire implanted in the people. Our insular position, our self-sufficing land, the vast distance which separates us from peoples of a pushing and enterprising spirit, have allowed us, or forced us, until recently, to grow up as true children of our own soil: the mercurial and imitative genius of the race found its natural bent (and how charming and delightful a one!) in the direction of the beautiful and artistic. Now, however, all this is changed or changing—I much question whether for the better. Versatility, the quick perception of the beautiful, the subtle power of imitation : all these are a necessary part of the artistic temperament, but in the hands of the states- man and politician they are apt to become dangerous tools. What has so far in our breathless race helped to save us from danger is—I smile to say it, though true enough—our appreciation and love of the grotesque for its own sake. This, if it be in art our most facile and delightful error, may in the development of Western institutions and customs turn out our merit and our safeguard. There is without doubt a full flavour of the grotesque in our recent headlong course of development, and a just perception thereof scattered broadcast among the people at large, as distinct from the young Japan party : where good-natured laughter reigns, danger fears to raise his hideous head. It is rampant desire and hunger-eyed expectation which, when they accompany change, lead to disaster ; for what change in custom or policy does not disappoint the makers of it ? With us there has been much that is childish, wonder-eyed and mirth-moving in the history of these latter years, in the somewhat infantile game which we have been playing.

An " England of the East " you speak of, in one of your letters written, on your way through the Mediterranean, of which you give me a pretty summer's-day picture. Yes, material interests in view, the notion is seductive. A variable climate, an extensive sea-board, good harbours, a maritime population, artisan dexterity, abundance of coal, etc.,—all these are ours, all these make the notion plausible. But against this you have to set the striking difference in character between the two people. The English are eminently a business nation, with a keen eye and correct judgment in commercial matters. We *may* become a business nation, but our natural tendency is artistic. The striking quality of the English people is, in my eyes, their power of self-restraint, their reluctance to undertake more than they feel they can carry out. We, on the other hand, could not have accomplished what we have save in the absence of this quality. The national temperament is impulsive. Our position in the East, too, is radically different from that of the English in the West. We are the leading, because the moving people of the East. Save in the merchant way, England has never led the West—never really aspired to do so. England is enterprising, not venturesome. She has never led the West as France led it, as Germany is now leading. She has never had to pay the penalty of leadership. She has been content with moderate ambitions. To this is due—as much as, or perhaps more than, to her insular position—her happy immunity from the crushing blows which have at times struck down into the dust of defeat her more ambitious sisters.

LETTER XVII.

LONDON, *January* 10*th*, 1889.

OVER here, and, I take it, in Europe generally, the spirit of inquiry, ranging from mere idle and diffuse curiosity to methodical and concentrated specu- lation, is of all things the most noteworthy to me. As a stranger, I find myself an object of vacant outward curiosity to the foolish, of grim inward speculation to the wise. You cannot well figure to yourself how pleasantly my path of inquiry is levelled and widened by the easy merit I have of being Japanese. I make acquaintances with quite astonishing facility. Ever on the alert for a new sensation, for anything which may decorously lift them up out of the dull rut of fashionable inter- course, the plutocratic aristocracy are more acces- sible to a stranger than I could have believed possible. With our own aristocracy, living as they yet do for the most part in dignified isolation, to be a stranger is to be nobody—here, to be a stranger is to be somebody. Provided you intro- duce yourself under the ægis of some well-known member of society, who thus silently vouches for your respectability, you are received with open arms and the most polite but discreet appearance of interest. The degree of respectability which is expected of you and with which you are credited when received is not burdensome; it entails nothing more than the observance of those social usages common to all civilised people, and doubtless includes a tacit assurance that no special precautions need be taken with regard to spoons, forks and other portable and interesting articles of value. As a foreigner, your character, your morals—except as matters of philosophical speculation—are not the object of inconvenient scrutiny. What is secretly expected of you is that you shall amuse, interest, astonish for a passing hour. It is rare, however, that you are received intimately. The good sense which is at bottom an abiding characteristic of this people, and which, if you look below the surface, is nowhere more developed than in this class, draws a very rigid line between casual acquaintanceship and intimacy. I have nevertheless had the good fortune to make one or two friends for myself—I have seen something of English family life. In essentials it is not very unlike ours. Quite recently I spent a few days in an English country house, and found my visit very pleasant. What struck me most was the true sense of hospitality possessed by my host and hostess. In all they did there was a veiled but very real concern that their guests should truly be, not merely seem, comfortable. Your habits, tastes, peculiarities are discreetly divined rather than openly inquired into. The request for privacy and individual liberty is pushed to an extreme which verges on the apparently discourteous : the manifest desire being that you should feel entirely free to dispose of yourself and of your time in the manner most agreeable to you. Withal there is a real if ungraceful courtliness of disposition, and a tolerance of, or even indifference to, individual characteristics. This latter trait, indeed, leads to overmuch dulness of conversation, which more often than not depends for its sprightliness on an amicable conflict of individual peculiarities of temperament and intellect.

In hotels, railway trains, theatres, and the many places where people unknown to each other are brought temporarily into contact, the average Englishman whom you meet is heavy and uninteresting. His tendency is at the outset to regard a stranger, whether belonging to his own country or another, rather as a possible enemy than as a possible friend,—at best he appears indifferent; his bearing implies, in effective but inarticulate manner: "I do not so much object to your presence as tolerate it." He is suspicious of a plausible, even of a pleasant, address. If by chance he enters into conversation with you it is commonly with the air rather of conferring a favour than of receiving one.

I paid a visit some days ago to the Houses of Parliament. Like all buildings in this part of the world, these are too massive, heavy and commonplace, too unrelieved in detail to please our taste. We miss the lightness of construction, the ingenuity of design, the wealth and finish of decoration which characterise our public buildings. Nowhere in Europe, or, for that matter, in the wide world, are there any constructions which have any pretension to rivalry in these respects with the wonders of Nikko. It must be admitted, nevertheless, that these vast stone fabrics of Europe are not without a certain grandeur. They strike us much as the huge remains of ancient Egypt, no doubt, strike the modern European: as things which, in their time and place, and in an order of ideas now fast disappearing, were worthy of admiration. But the world has outgrown the barbaric idea of splendour; Europeans themselves have given proof of this in the avidity with which they have thrown themselves upon our art products, and in their painstaking and earnest efforts to learn the lessons which it is in our power to teach them.

The temple (Westminster Abbey) which stands near to and on the north side of the Houses of Parliament, is a more favourable specimen than they are of Western architecture, but the real beauty and noble if bald simplicity of its interior are marred by the Western mania of crowding together in a restricted space a multiplicity of works of art, which fatigue the eye and distract the attention. Statuary is a branch of art in which we are ignorant : I will not attempt to pass judgment on the many marble figures and monuments which fill the temple; I restrict myself to the bare statement that the greater part of them failed to please me, and that in general I would have wished them away, not as ugly in themselves, but as too numerous and cumbersome.

The exterior of the Houses of Parliament is more impressive, more worthy of the "mother of Parliaments" than the halls in which is discussed the business of the nation. The House of Commons is disappointing : merely a very large room or oblong hall with benches on either side running in the direction of its length, a wide passage down the middle with a table at one end of it, and opposite the end of the table the chair of the speaker or president. Above all this runs a gallery round the four walls, where the representatives of the press are accommodated, and where strangers, furnished with a permit, are admitted to listen to the debates. It does not appear that the public readily avails itself of this privilege. The members, to my surprise, sit about in a very unbusinesslike manner, and, when not asleep, appear to pay attention to anybody or anything rather than to the person who happens to be addressing them. They also usually wear their hats in the room, perhaps as a token of their independence—to which possession it may have been necessary to sacrifice that of courtesy. This astonished me; but to understand my astonishment you must not forget that in this the comparison lies between Western heads and Eastern feet. But this comparison is in itself somewhat discourteous; perhaps you will remind me that, in the Western phrase, " evil communications corrupt good manners."

LETTER XVIII.

TOKIO, *January 20th*, 1889.

THIS morning I rose from my bed with what my doctor calls a chill on the liver. It is certain that the desire to put one's finger on the faults of things and the follies of men has been beneficently implanted in man's bosom, in order that he may be goaded forward and may goad others forward in the path of progress and amelioration. This is perhaps the *raison d'être* of the bilious and splenetic conditions, in which it is observable that this desire is greatly sharpened, and the length, strength and capacity of the said finger proportionately increased, so that it is not merely prone to point to sore places, but to prod them, and excite them to a state of healthy activity, in which the growth of a surface skin, beneath which the evil may grow unregarded, shall be rendered impossible. This short preamble is merely to warn you that I am in a fault-finding mood, and that I am going to find fault, not, my dear friend, with you, but with *your* friend, the ubiquitous European.

96

I distrust the European, his modes and his procedures. In my present mood I incline more to vehement assertion than to the giving of reasons, and I chafe under the despotism of common sense, which opposes the course of my inclination. I distrust the European then, first and foremost, because he is too practical: the practical man being, as a rule, one whose attention is so exclusively fixed on means, that the end for which alone those means are of value is often entirely neglected and even lost sight of. I need scarcely pause to point out that the end is the man's well-being, under whatever form—the man's happiness. I may be replied to, on this head, that the means are at the same time the end; that in the energetic acquisitiveness of the man, not in the acquisition of the thing, be it love, power, or riches, lies the end itself. I say "no" to such sophistical reasoning. I will admit that the end embraces the means, but no more. For whatever pleasure there may be, and is, in acquiring, you cannot gainsay that you acquired, in order that you may use; and in right use is the main element of happiness. Acquire eagerly, not pausing to reflect how you shall use, and you will find yourself weighted with a burden rather than blessed with a possession. This is the fault I have to find with the Europeans whom I know. They are all eagerness to acquire. They will not pause to consider how to use well that which they have. In eagerness there is

7

pleasure, but this disappears as eagerness verges
on anxiety, which it is in its very nature to do,
and for happiness there is necessary some degree
of rest, of composure.

My knowledge of European countries mainly
rests, of course, on hearsay and book-learning, so
that I merely hazard the observation that there is, in
those countries, a larger residuum of misery than in
ours, because in the former the race for advancement
is more arduous and absorbing, the individual more
spendthrift of himself and more reckless of his real
well-being, with the result that in the rear of the
race there is found a disorganised mob of persons,
bankrupt in health, happiness and pocket.   I
found myself, too, on the remarks of observant
foreigners who visit our country.   Most of these
are impressed with the good humour, the genial
bonhomie, the smiling and happy appearance of
our people.   You, in one of your recent letters to
me, bear witness unconsciously to the justness of
this remark, by your observation on the general
look of preoccupation, of care and of anxiety which
so forcibly struck you as characteristic of the people
on your arrival in England.

The disordered imagination and topsy-turvydom
of judgment which I suspect in our European
friends finds a parallel in the strange contrariness
and awkwardness of many of their manual practices
—I do not speak of mechanical talent, which I
freely concede to them.   The European carpenter,

for instance, or other artisan, with his voluminous
tool-chest and paraphernalia of ingenious imple-
ments, is frequently outdone in rapid, dexterous
and delicate hand-work, by our artisan with the
half-dozen simple tools he has at command, tools
which he has generally made almost entirely himself. The awkwardness of the foreign carpenter
is manifest in his slow and slovenly method of
work. For instance, he will always plane and frequently saw away from instead of towards himself,
the instrument thus held obstructing the close
superintendence by the eye of the work to be done.
With curious perversity Europeans make use of
right-handed in the place of left-handed screws;
yet the right hand has a surer and steadier twisting
power from right to left than from left to right.
Similarly, it is easier to shoot a bolt into its lock
by turning the key from right to left, than the
opposite way. European locks, however, are almost
invariably made on the contrary method. In the
manual art of book-making it is, I believe, the
common practice to place the author's or editor's
notes at the bottom of the page, instead of, as with
us, at the top, whence the eye can easily and
naturally run down the text again to the point at
which the break occurred, instead of retracing its
way backwards. Even in such trifling matters as
the address of a letter the wrongheadedness of
European methods is apparent. The information
required by the post-office employés is not given

in the order wanted, but in the reverse order.
Most of these matters are in themselves trivial,
—they are of no more weight than smoke; but,
like smoke, they serve to show the direction of
the wind.

Passing from the utilitarian to the artistic, there
is observable the same incompetence to distinguish
between the end and the means, the same gross
indifference to the distinction. Thus the European
custom, pursued both in public and in private, of
collecting and herding together in a confined space
a confused number of artistic objects is evidence
that the means of pleasing the sense for the beautiful is confounded with the pleasure itself. The
attention is distracted and the critical faculty dazed
by the presence of a number of beautiful objects
in close juxtaposition ; the artistic sense is blunted,
the keen edge of its appreciation taken off. Any
work of beauty—be it even in the deft arrangement
and combination of half a dozen flowers—requires
in the beholder, in order to his full enjoyment
and understanding of it, the absence of distracting
and competing emotions. Undivided attention,
trained observation, concentrated and renewed, are
necessary in order that he may seize all the subtle
points of beauty which the artist has delicately and
lovingly put, sometimes only hinted, in his work.
The custom of our art-lovers in keeping the bulk
of their treasures stowed away out of sight, and
exposing only one or two artistic objects at a time,

until the sense has seized and grown dull for the moment to their beauty, is one which excites astonishment in our European acquaintances,—a further proof, were one required, that with them the parade and' pride of possession is more than possession itself.

LETTER XIX.

PARIS, *February 7th*, 1889.

So you see I have left England, but only for a trip to Paris, whence I shall very shortly return. Did you ever meet —— at Tokio? The minister of war sent him off two years back to study the organisation of the French army. The French Government very courteously gave him an honorary commission, and attached him to the staff of the general commanding the *corps d'armée* stationed at Paris. He is a very bright, intelligent fellow, and has the *entrée* to much of the best society in the capital, so that although I have been here barely a fortnight I have already done and seen much.

Paris is a smaller, brighter London, more ornate but less picturesque. There is a general sense of liveliness as distinct from hurry, very noticeable after London. The weather is brighter, the sun shines more clearly, the contrast of light and shade is bolder, and more trenchant the line which separates them. The people are more mercurial, laughter-loving, affable and gay than those on the other side of the Channel; pleasanter, I find, in the general commerce of life, less trustworthy, perhaps, in the more intimate relations,—but of this my experience is too limited to judge. The difference (or some of it) between the two nations is instantly manifest on comparing the French with the English PRESS. I write the word in big letters, out of respect for the largeness and importance of the thing, not for its intrinsic worth. The Press, where free in Europe, is the mirror of the national mind, the unconscious exponent of the virtues and vices, the wisdom and folly, the humours, peculiarities and distortions of the average inhabitant (*l'homme sensuel moyen,* as a French writer has it) of the region. A Frenchman who knows England will tell you of the English Press that it is dull; an Englishman who knows France will say of the French Press that it is licentious and ill-informed. To the average man's mind there is undoubtedly a connection between dulness and order, as also between licence and anarchy. The leading English newspapers are remarkable for the extent and precision of their information on current affairs, and for a certain solid or even stolid common sense. The French papers, on the contrary, are careless of news, which they not infrequently invent or admit from sources which are not genuine, and which, even when genuine, are often tainted; but they are amusing, witty and sparkling.

As to society, the general constitution of the

classes presents no very marked difference from that of England. The two countries nevertheless afford the observer a notable contrast in the position and importance of the aristocracy. In England every noble is wealthy, but in France many a baron or count possesses little else besides his title, which he uses as a beggar uses his rags, to hide his nakedness. In England, peers are often found in high political and official places; in France rarely. As a class the French nobility exercises absolutely no influence on politics. A section of it has gathered itself together in a particular quarter of Paris, and there busies itself with the concoction of infantile plots—on paper—for the restoration of the monarchy. It corresponds with the exiled prince, and, by remaining obstinately fixed within a narrow circle of ideas, by keeping itself studiously ignorant of the tendencies of the country, by making much of every item of news favourable to its hopes, and turning a deaf ear to news of other kinds, it occasionally galvanises itself into a spasm of belief that the return of the king is at hand. The king may return, indeed, but if he does it will be owing rather to the mistakes of his enemies than to the exertions of his friends.

From the point of view of politics, the Paris artisan is an important person. In an airy, light-hearted, irresponsible, but occasionally vehement mood and manner, he lays down the law (which includes the overthrowing of it) for Paris, and Paris lays down the law for the country. Like our own working man the Paris artisan is a hard worker and a skilful, yet gay, pleasure-seeker, and of a mocking spirit. But between the two there is little inner likeness, only outward resemblance. The mockery of our people is gentle—founded, I take it, on a good-humoured, more or less unconscious perception of the unavoidable incongruities and inequalities of life. That of the French is inclement, and rests mainly on a resentful, fully conscious apprehension of these incongruities and inequalities. The flavour of the one is acidulous, of the other bitter. .

The Paris artisan believes in nothing, submits all things in conflict to the arbitrament of a crude compound of sentiment and surface logic, and accepts the resulting conclusions with the most astounding and light-hearted facility. This spirit is a heritage of the great revolution which shook the foundations of the Western world, and which, in this country, swept away all but the name of tradition. For tradition the Paris artisan has absolutely no respect: it is an encumbrance, a hindrance to the free development of reason, a provokingly inert obstruction to the fulfilment of the affections and desires implanted by Nature in the breast of man. It could not occur to him that tradition, as an embodiment of past experience, might be a useful guide to conduct and conviction, because primarily, according to him, wrong

conduct and absurd conviction is the experience
of the past.   Still less could it occur to him that
human government, both personal and political,
is purely empirical, dependent, for its proper application to changing circumstances, on the right
understanding of the long and ceaseless conflict
between use and abuse, reason and unreason;
because to him it is a matter of *a priori* certainty
that existing institutions are built up on the abuse
and unreason of the past; so that, while believing
ourselves to be standing firmly on our feet, we are
in reality most ludicrously standing on our heads,
and perceiving the world upside down.   Such is
the conviction of the radical Paris artisan.

The European radical, of whom the more intelligent Paris artisan is probably an average specimen,
has a nose for the trace of a taint in governments
and administrations as keen as the bloodhound's
for the trail of a criminal.   Wherever held properly
in leash his use is apparent, but as things now are
the leash is often in forceless hands, and, the
quarry overtaken, it becomes a matter of difficulty
and danger to whip the animal off it.

Looking over the last letter I have received
from you, I am tempted to say a word or two in
defence of young Japan.   But, even though I
should stand on your ground and endeavour to
look through your eyes, I could not see quite as
you do.   If "let us enjoy to-day, for to-morrow we
are not," or, as they put it over here, "let us eat,

drink, and be merry, for to-morrow we die," be really the ultimate fruit of our philosophy, why not pluck it ? Happiness, as has often been observed, and as you repeat, is the aim of the individual. If this is the way to happiness, why not choose it ? Why should the individual trouble himself about posterity, about the future ? Let posterity and the future take care of themselves,—I suspect we can do them harm only by first doing harm to ourselves.

This is the kind of reasoning I have sometimes listened to on such matters. I need scarcely say it does not satisfy me, but I do not very well know why. From the moment the search for happiness is made the ruling consideration of the individual's existence, to the exclusion of the consideration of duty, I scarcely see what is to be said against such reasoning. Now, the idea of duty as ruling a man's life is antiquated. One must be of one's time, or nothing. I acknowledge that I ought not to care about posterity, but I do. I suppose I am hope-lessly illogical in feeling ; or it may be that I am not yet sufficiently imbued with the spirit of what you name young Japan.

LETTER XX.

YASHIRI TO TOKIWARA.

TOKIO, *February 8th*, 1889.

FOR the last twenty years or more, ideas of a constitution, of representative institutions, and of parliamentary government, have been in the air. Every discerning man, therefore, seeing from which quarter the wind set, has kept his eyes turned towards Europe—especially, I think, towards England. It must be admitted that the Government has taken much pains to collect information, and that the framing of the new constitution displays a fairly creditable compromise between the passion for symmetry which informs constitution-makers, and the practical common sense which recognises that men are not abstract entities, but concrete and mostly troublesome realities. It is not possible to foresee what ulterior consequences these changes carry in their train; but the disquiet of the free European nations, their feverish, unsettled, restless condition, does not fill me with any great confidence in the future of our own.

Gradually, very gradually, a suspicion has taken

shape in my mind that there is in representative institutions and parliamentary government something of the nature of a solemn farce, unconsciously played by the political public, secretly recognised as such, and fostered, for reasons of their own, by the political leaders. The great mass of men in every country is perennially under the influence of the belief that, whenever anything is wrong in the condition or in the affairs of the country, it is within the competence of government to put the wrong thing right. Political leaders, on the other hand, versed in state affairs, well know how difficult, and often how impossible it is to substitute a right thing for a wrong without bringing about, in the change, some evil, generally unforeseen, which turns out on trial to outweigh the benefit conferred. The tendency of the masses, then, is in the direction of legislation, that of the responsible leaders in the direction of political inactivity, or merely of political show, smoke and froth. So it comes about—at least in England, it seems to me—that the semblance of legislation is always fussily present, but that very little of importance or permanent value finds its way into the statute-book.

It appears to me that between the principal men of the two English political parties there must be, as it were, a secret or tacit understanding, an unwritten compact, that the people shall be humoured with the shadow of legislation, but deprived of the substance of it; that a puppet show, decorous if possible, but amusing at all hazards, shall be provided for their entertainment, with the object of distracting their attention from supposititious, or real but immedicable ills. I notice that each party, while in opposition, exerts itself strenuously to prevent the party in office from legislating with effect, irrespectively of the goodness or badness of any particular proposal. The party in power, on the other hand, while affecting impatience of the opposition, appears to be secretly relieved at being prevented from committing itself to anything drastic or definite. Each party, while in opposition, seeks to affix discredit to the government by accusing it of ineptitude and of indifference to legislation, and, when in power, attempts to shelter itself by charging the other side with factiousness and obstruction. Thus, while patriotically avoiding legislation, both parties flourish their standards, sound their clarions, charge and countercharge in a mimic warfare which, to the masses, presents the appearance of being real. Every one concerned is, I suppose, tolerably satisfied : the politicians with their share of office, salaries, patronage and importance ; the masses (whose memory is so short and whose nature in things political is so inconstant that there is never a pause to recollect what politicians who are in said when out, and what politicians who are out said when they wanted to remain in) with the energetic inactivity of their leaders and representatives.

When by chance I consult the principal papers of the English press on some political question which divides them, I find it difficult to rid myself of the impression that there is no real matter in debate between them, but only a political play or farce in course of representation, the actors of which no more believe in their parts than do those few spectators, whose freedom from prejudice enables them to derive especial amusement from the show. I take up one after another of these party organs, and I find in the written word no evidence of internal conviction, but only of the desire to convince or hoodwink others ; no genuine belief in the thing advocated nor real distrust of the thing decried, but merely belief or distrust professionally instilled into the minds of those politically-minded readers for whom the paper is specially designed. When the matter under discussion happens to be one, not of opinion, but of fact, the farce broadens. Some incident occurs which bears strongly on the political question of the hour, and which is plainly creditable or damaging to one or other of the two political parties. Each paper, according to its political persuasion or profession, relates the occurrence, the incident, the fact ; but with so great a subordination to the discipline of party in the relation, that among them the fact becomes as one of those abstract metaphysical terms which represent different things to different persons. Nevertheless, as each journal gives that version of the fact which suits its readers best, the political necessities of party and the common obligation of honesty do not get too widely sundered ; for, from among them, the independent inquirer may, by taking trouble and comparing versions, arrive at the truth of the matter, while the partisan, indifferent to this particular, obtains his evidence as he wishes to have it—ready-made to suit his taste.

LETTER XXI.

PARIS, *February 20th*, 1889.

LIBERTÉ, EGALITÉ, FRATERNITÉ : this is the motto of the great republic. A lovely day it was, as the train glided with me into Paris. Sunbright and joyful the weather, heartful and gay my mood, as I issued from the railway terminus and my wondering glance fell on these three brave words—stretching in huge painted letters along a high wall, which, some hundred feet away, faces the station exit. Brave and soul-stirring words, which came upon me as a sudden and joyous revelation of glorious possibilities ! The people who thronged the streets, too, seemed, as it were, to smile the words forth from their bright, amiable, cheerful faces : " See, we are brothers, equal in mutual love one for the other, free in mutual respect for the freedom each of the other." An idle motive of curiosity prompted me to ask what this high unbroken wall surrounded. I was told : one of the state prisons. The answer seemed to give me a slight chill.—Surely, a cloud had stolen over the face of the sun.   And were these men, or marion- ettes, whom I beheld ? genuine men and women, smiling real assent to real things, or mere manikins, posturing and grimacing on a stage my own sight too dull to trace the strings leading down below it ?

Men, or marionettes? How often, and in how many different ways, have I asked myself that question !—answering it now this way and now that. To bed in the evening under conviction of marionettehood, up the following morning most obviously and potently a man. But what, you will ask, has all this to do with the great republican motto ? and what, in sober reality, does the great republican motto mean? " Liberty "—excellent ; but liberty to be or become what ? to do what ? "Equality"—good, very good; but equality of whom, and in what directions or particulars ? " Fraternity" —ought this not rather to come first, as a message of peace and love, from which, duly hearkened to, must assuredly follow whatever is possible or desirable in the other two ?

I made it my business to inquire of various persons what they understood by these words under present conditions. One said: liberty for the Jews and financiers, in confraternity of rascal- dom, to rob the French people of their savings, with equality of immunity before the law. Another: liberty of conscience for those who have none, equality in religious *no*-instruction, fraternity . . . . here he stuttered indignantly, his imagination failing before the enormity of the thing to be described. A third shrugged his shoulders—one of the most expressive and impressive answers I received. But all were not thus minded. Of other answers given me, one was to this effect : that the motto represents an ideal towards which, amid many turmoils and troubles, the nation was steadily advancing. Liberty for every man to prosecute his own affairs with the least possible intervention from government; equality of all men before the law ; fraternity between all men obeying the law—a text on which might be preached a long sermon. I had some secret amusement out of a pompous pedant, who volunteered to explain that the equality affirmed was of rights, "all men being born with equal inalienable rights." But when I came to inquire what were exactly these "equal inalienable rights," we began to get into the shifting sands of argument, from which I withdrew with what skill I could, my own private but silent conclusion being that a man's rights are merely certain advantages or facilities which society secures to him on condition that he will fulfil certain tasks and observe certain rules, which may be summed up under the idea of duties ; both rights and duties being matters which depend on time, clime and circumstance.

A neat comment on what would appear the most natural of all rights—the right of a man to live—

is furnished by an anecdote told of a celebrated French diplomatist and statesman, who, on reproving a notorious scamp for certain shady transactions, was met by the observation, "Well, your Excellency, a man must live!" "I do not see the necessity," replied the statesman.

In these Western lands the kind of equality which men have most steadfastly, and, at times, most passionately striven for—nay, even died for, is the equality of all men before the law; and this, notably in the three most advanced European powers, has now practically been attained. The common sense of people has in general revolted against the monstrous absurdity of the fiction that men are born free and equal. And it is reflection over this monstrous absurdity itself which will in turn make men suspect that formal equality before the law cannot be the last word of wisdom in jurisprudence, the ultimate and most perfect form to which human justice may in time be moulded. For myself, I cannot but believe this equality to be a new point of departure, a coign of vantage whence securely to survey the path to a true *in*equality before the law which shall serve the ends of a far more perfect and therefore nobler justice.

Among the half-educated and shallow-minded, especially, the vague but dogmatic assertion of the theoretical equality of men and of their rights is very common. It is, from one point of view, a source of continual astonishment to me. That

such an idea should take root in the soil of the
Celestial Empire, for instance, is not easy to
imagine ; but if it did, we might expect it to grow
—the intense conservatism and essential unprogres-
siveness of the Chinese lending itself to the death
in life of general equality.   But that this flower, or
rather weed, should not only be of Western origin,
but actually thrive there, is, when well considered,
surely a most remarkable fact.   The social constitution and prevalent tendency of these countries is
absolutely hostile to such an ideal.   The history of
their material development is a tale condensed from
millions of others : the stories of countless disparate
individual growths.   The plasticity of their social
aggregates, compared with those of Eastern countries, is a direct and unmistakable effect of the
unfettered play of individual differences, tendencies
and powers.   There is not perhaps a greater degree
of inequality among men in Europe now than there
was of old, but there is a greater variety of kind.
The tendency is not so much to accentuate existing
inequalities as to develop fresh ones.   No observer
born and bred out of Europe can fail to be struck
by this.   It runs through not only the material
order of things, but the mental and moral.   To an
Oriental, the multiplicity of opinions, the conflict
of convictions on any and every matter of belief,
speculation and conduct, is nothing less than
amazing.   It is a disintegrating force of the first
order, a solvent of existing forms.   Presently, when

the era of huge armaments shall have passed away, it will begin powerfully to influence the sentiment of nationality, which has its roots in the conscious-ness o the necessity of solidarity for effective offence and defence.

LETTER XXII.

TOKIO, *February 26th,* 1889.

YOUR remarks concerning the significance of the middle classes of society in Europe seem to me well-founded. I think you are very likely right in the estimate you make of the part played by them in the change from the feudal to the industrial organisation of the Western nations. But in such matters it is by no means easy to distinguish between cause and effect. What you say at all events confirms me yet more in my opinion that we are in far too great a hurry with our reforms at home.

My father, (rest be his in the favour of the gods!) I have ever held sacredly in my memory as a wise and good man. He was, indeed, a man of excellent understanding and judgment, so that my respect for him grew continually from the time when I could first comprehend what these qualities are and what they are worth. But do you not think this very right respect would have stood confused and shamefaced if, arrived at manhood, I had with pride proceeded to don my equipment

119

of Samurai,[1] only to find—to my distress—that my excellent and well-intentioned father had had it made for me years before, in anticipation of my manhood, and that now, putting it on me, I found it either too large or too small? So, I fear, it may presently be with us, that, standing in the midst of confusion, we shall think with sorrow and bitterness of our well-meaning but not overwise party of progress, now so busily engaged in preparing the fine clothes and the shining armour of this infant civilisation's maturer years.

So far, it is true, things have gone fairly well with us since the restoration. Fast as we have been moving, we have as yet had no serious fall, not even a dangerous stumble. Our latest step,[2] indeed, has been made with a seven-league boot: more properly not a step, but rather a long leap from the noon-lit present into the clear-obscure of the future, where no one knows whether we shall alight on our feet or land insensible : foolish head against unespied rock. You will have seen all about that memorable day in the newspapers which reached you by the last mail. The popular enthusiasm and rejoicing intoxicated even old grey heads like mine. Most remarkable of all was the

[1] *Samurai:* the feudal retainers of the Daimios, or great territorial lords; many of the Samurai were lesser nobles.

[2] The new constitution of Japan was promulgated by the Mikado on February 11th, 1889.—ED.

character of the decorations and legends which everywhere marked the imperial path, and attested, strongly as such things can attest, to the love and reverence of the people for the throne and their devotion to its present occupant. But with the next morning came sober reflection, and with reflection misgiving. I recalled, not without a slight shudder, what I had read of the boundless confidence of the French people in the unfortunate Louis XVI. at the time of the National Convention, and of their enthusiastic good feeling towards him, and then that these very people, gay, good-humoured and happy-tempered as our own, shortly proceeded to cut off his head. I do not mean to suggest that there is any true parallelism between the two sets of circumstances; I merely note how often forecasts differ widely from results.

And what shall we make of our three hundred ?[1] More dubious still, what will our three hundred make of us? The Upper House I do not so much trouble myself about. There is here some guarantee of efficiency. Men whose business it has been to administer, to govern, may not possess any great technical skill in the making of laws, but we may expect them to be at least familiar with the conditions under which laws are likely to work. Experience will whisper to them : Such and such a law is likely to be good, bad or indifferent; is at

[1] The lower house of representatives, which is to consist of three hundred members.—ED.

all events one which it is possible or impossible practically to apply.   Experience of men and affairs will suggest to them : quash this or that ingenious verbal embodiment of a mere abstract *to be,* hopelessly irreconcilable with what actually *is.*   But what I should much like to learn from our constitution-mongers is where they propose to find the fit men for our lower house.   Three hundred individuals they will doubtless get : I could find them myself to-day in the streets of Tokio, with plenty of sinew and skill to guide a rikisha.   But the fortunes of an empire ?—a very different matter this.   Between the old daimio class and the rural population, what material is there fit to be worked up into a representative assembly of any value ?   The Samurai ?   Excellent, honourable men for the most part, but still essentially fighting men, not legists.   On your own showing, the kind of men we require should in a great measure be drawn from the better intellects to be found in an intelligent, hard-working middle-class, men conversant with the general principles of organisation and skilful in the dovetailing of details.   These men are not easily found except in large and populous towns : pray recollect that with a population of some thirty-eight millions we have no more than five towns whose inhabitants number over ten thousand.   Remember, too, that in every newly constituted popular assembly there will be found a goodly number of apparently clever and certainly vain persons who, casting overboard the sure ballast of experience and spreading wide sail to the shifting and delusive wind of theory, draw after them into their wake of danger the more foolish, unstable and volatile spirits.   It is of course a very different matter with assemblies of long standing, experienced in the practical work of legislation.   Such persons as I have just described could scarcely find a seat in the British House of Commons.   There is a crumb of comfort in the hope that possibly we may find some useful men among those who have served in the assemblies elected under the restricted scheme of local government.   These have been at work now more than ten years, and on the whole their work has proved satisfactory.   But I expect little from these local assemblies as affording education for the fit discharge of legislative affairs. The mental horizon of the men who compose them does not expand rapidly ; the national assembly, of which they will probably form a part, may prove to be as useless and unfit as the two we have already had, in which case its end will not unlikely be as abortive as theirs, and more harm than good will have come of the experiment.

The truth is, that no population is fit for representative institutions and parliamentary government which has not been growing in the will and ability to wrest these little by little from the iron hand of personal rule.   The observation, I know, is trite, but it is none the less true.   So far as I am aware, this system has nowhere been established on lines of power and permanence, save in those countries where of their own strength the people have made themselves masters of the situation. To my mind, it is scarcely an extravagant parallel to say that for the Mikado to decree that on some particular date the Japanese people shall proceed freely to govern themselves, say, like the English, is something like the president of the Royal Academy in London decreeing that in future the English people shall display the love of art and exercise the instinctive artistic judgment which characterise all classes of our population. The right of self-government is one of those which, in practice, are rights only in so far as they are mights. You cannot properly confer it on a people ; the people must seize it of their own initiative, not necessarily through violence or bloodshed, but by their own desire and through their own capacity. If, as you think, industry and commerce prepared the nations of the West for the exercise of it, let us turn our attention first to the growth of industry and the expansion of commerce, the rest will follow. Meanwhile the hot-headed zeal of some of the more advanced members of the *Kaishinto*[1] leaves me sorely afraid that, in the parlance and occasionally the practice of the West, we are about to try the making of bricks without straw.

[1] The advanced party in politics.—ED.

TOKIWARA TO YASHIRI.

PARIS, *March 6th*, 1889.

No man knows to what degree of perfection can be carried the art of polite conversation until he has been introduced to French society. I do not speak of the talk of a literary coterie, nor of that of what I will call—for want of a better expression —a professedly intellectual circle, but of the general conversation of well-bred persons. In England, as in France, you meet with clever people, learned people, people with a distinctly original turn of mind—of the last perhaps more in England than in France. But while in the former country a pleasant talker is the exception which proves the rule of dulness, in the latter a dull talker is the exception to the rule of quickness and sprightliness. Here the form of speech is always neat, the speech itself always to the point, whether the point be worth attention or not. Doubtless a Frenchman is a more gregarious animal than his over-sea neighbour—which fact may in some measure account for the differences between them in conversational ability; but, at bottom, the real reason of the Frenchman's excellence in this matter is to be found in an inbred, consuming desire to please, to charm, to entertain, and a capacity for taking trouble to that end. In polite French society, the play of conversation keeps your mind constantly on the alert, induces a febrile condition which, with the untrained, is apt to engender fatigue. The success of this kind of entertainment is in direct proportion to the capacity of those present for throwing a quick succession of coloured lights on the momentary subject of conversation. The steady white beam of inquiry is not tolerated, because above all things you must avoid going to the heart of any matter. Your business is to give brilliancy to the surface—varnish, mostly, which comes off with ease, and is with equal ease replaced. From flower to flower flies the nimble wit—but as the butterfly, not as the bee. Whenever and wherever you can, make your point; let it be fine, if possible, but thrust at all hazards. When, as will sometimes happen, you cannot readily find something clever to say, cleverly say something, to the accompaniment of an arch, knowing look, meaning "this is the genuine article": it is ten to one the others will take your look for your word. I have met here men and women whose real powers barely remove them from stupidity, but who can call up this bright look to perfection,—you would think they absolutely overflowed with cleverness, but when you get home and think it all over quietly—well, it will not bear thinking over.

In England there is in conversation more of repose, less than nothing of the French nimbleness, of the French *esprit*. The borrowing from over-sea such words as *causerie, bon mot, jeu d'esprit, esprit d'àpropos,* indicates native poverty of expression in light social conversation, which may be characterised as orderly, amiable and usually uninteresting. You are not called on to make efforts ; and this, at all events, is a compensation. Not the only one, either : there is none of the after-taste of disappointment left by sham cleverness. In general, conversation in England is so uniformly, so genuinely and frankly dull, that at least you are under no risk of confounding the diamond's flash with the bubble's glitter. Why is there this marked difference between the two societies ? Whence the keener desire to shine, to please, on this side of the Channel than-on the other ? I set it down to the surface vanity of the Frenchman. The immediate praise of his fellows, their quick recognition of his good points, are sweeter to him, more immediately necessary to his self-esteem, than is the case with the Englishman. The latter is a proud man, often with a false pride ; the former is a vain one, but his vanity is rarely offensive, and, at times, is not without a certain element of charm. A

Frenchman likes to be praised openly. Praise an Englishman to his face, and it will make him uncomfortable. Let a Frenchman suspect, as in general he will, that you scarcely think as well of him as your words convey, and he will shrug his shoulders as a private protest against your judgment. Let an Englishman suspect this, and he will be inclined to avoid you or drop your acquaintance. Vanity on the one side, pride and sensitiveness on the other. The Englishman makes an idol of his self-esteem ; the Frenchman worships, in the enchanted mirror of flattery, what appears there as his own image.

But the difference between the island "upper ten thousand " and the French *beau-monde* is not altogether explicable by means of a direct comparison of individual characteristics. Circumstances bound up in the historical development of the two nations have had not a little to do with bringing about this difference. The French revolution not only shattered the political fabric of the country, but affected in a very marked manner that most conservative of all institutions : the division of the people into distinct social castes. The basis of reconstruction was Napoleon's famous " *La carrière ouverte au talent.*" Talent of this or that kind became a natural passport into this or that coveted place. Society, the *beau-monde* itself, became permeated with the idea, so that, within certain wide and ill-defined limits, and under elastic conditions, talent came to serve as a key to the jealously-bolted gate of high caste.

In England there is a not ill-grounded distrust of mere talent, talent unaccompanied by other qualities. And then, looking at the nation as a whole, it has managed its affairs with caution. Society was not suddenly apprised that it had been sitting on a gunpowder barrel by the application of a lighted match to its contents. Alive in good time to the danger which threatened them, the upper classes considerately made room on the powder barrel, and invited the sometimes well-intentioned but careless persons with a turn for experiments to come and sit thereon with them. The English aristocracy has known how and when to surrender its exclusive privileges to the nation. But the English aristocracy is nevertheless human, —it has its vanities and its foibles. Prudence and common sense dictated the abandonment of a large share of political power, but the social prestige which rested on it—that was another matter. The great middle class had been steadily growing in political importance ; it was now the arbiter of the nation in political matters, and, day by day, was putting forth social pretensions. How was the exclusiveness dear to an upper class to be maintained ? Wealth, as a badge of position, was inadmissible : many of the middle class were very rich. The sole real distinction which remained was birth within the aristocratic order, but this was

9

a distinction by no means easy to apply. The system of primogeniture was necessarily accompanied by a progressive social degradation of younger sons and their posterities, thus rendering the line between aristocracy and middle class indefinite in regard to birth. It has thus come about in England that the upper class has informally enrolled itself as an order resembling that of the Freemasons—a freemasonry of fashion—in the sense that its members recognise one another by signs unknown to, or too subtle for recognition and imitation by, the general: an unmistakable but indescribable *flavour* in the mode of thought, in the manner of speech, in address and general bearing—quite distinct from, even alien to, mere cleverness, quickness or brightness. These latter qualities, it was felt, are not the birthright of any one class. Moreover, quick and clever persons are also not infrequently persons with an irrepressible talent for pushing themselves to the front. In a word, mere quickness and cleverness got to be looked at with suspicion in good society—especially by those who are neither quick nor clever—as being in a sense unsound, foreign to good breeding, incompatible with repose of manner and personal distinction.

LETTER XXIV.

ROME, *March* 16th, 1889.

I HAD intended to go no farther afield than Paris, but ——, who had long projected a journey to Italy, persuaded me to go with him. Why I have come to Rome, unless to please ——, who has pleased me, I do not know. The object of my journey to Europe, and especially to England, cannot well be furthered by my coming here—not but what Rome is of absorbing interest to the student of history. My present concern, however, is with the living phœnix, not with the ashes of the dead one. All those wonders of Rome's youth, then, and all those other wonders of her middle age, I will pass over in respectful and admiring silence. What could I say of them that has not already been said, and said so well? But if old Rome is dead to all I have come to learn, new Rome is not. The seat of the Pope, the religious centre of the Western world, is not a locality of slight interest. I need scarcely remind you that the Christians of Europe are divided into three

131

great sects, or camps : the Roman Catholics, the Protestants, and the Greek or Russian Church. "Camps," I said, and advisedly ; for, like all religious differences, these have led to battle, and the question of orthodoxy has more than once been put to the arbitrament of the sword.

Of these three great sects of the Christian religion, the most important is the Roman Catholic (that known to us until lately under the title "the religion of the Lord of Heaven") of which the Pope is the supreme head.   His power has diminished and his splendour has waned since the time of our famous embassy to Rome in the age of the Usurpers [1]; and the boast of the city is no longer that she is the spiritual mistress of the Western world, but the capital of the Italian nation.   Until quite lately the Pope was a temporal sovereign, reigning over a modest stretch of territory round about Rome known as the Papal Dominions.   But

[1] 1573—1603 : the interregnum between the Shôgunate of the Ashikaga and that of the Tokugawa, during which period the Christian religion made considerable progress in Japan. The celebrated Iyeyasu (founder of the latter line of Shôguns) projected and partially executed a series of reforms, among which was included the extirpation of Christianity.   His son and grandson followed in his footsteps, and by the end of the latter's reign the Christian religion had practically disappeared from the land.   It is interesting to notice that the policy of Iyeyasu and his immediate successors, in this respect, was prompted by motives in great measure resembling those which led to the rigid persecution of the Christians under certain of the Roman Emperors.—ED.

the heart of the Italians had long been set on fusing the separate states of the peninsula (some of them then under alien rule) into one nation and under one head—or at least one government, whether royal or republican. In brief, it came about that the Pope was deprived of his lands and of his capital, and at the present moment is lord only of his palace (the Vatican) and of his spiritual subjects. He, and, in general, the Roman Catholic Church, are indignant at this spoliation, declaring it to be impossible for him to carry out his work without fear or favour under present conditions: this, at least, is what their argument amounts to, although they do not put it quite so nakedly as I have. On the other hand, it is said by some that the spiritual authority of the Supreme Pontiff is more likely to gain than to lose by the disappearance of temporal power.

In view of the discussions which are now going on at home as to the advisability of favouring the propagation of the Christian religion in Japan, you will perhaps expect me to say something on the subject as it strikes me from here. At best I can but touch the fringe of the question. In the first place, as you know, I am by no means a partisan either of one side or of the other; either of those who advocate the claims of Christianity as the religion of the nations upon whom we are remoulding ourselves, or of the others whose contention is that we should take what of good the West may

have to give us and| throw|;aside whatever the
West may have of useless or effete.

I very much doubt whether we at home understand Christianity any better than the Christians
here understand Shintoism or Buddhism—notwithstanding that we have some practical experience
on our side. A few competent observers and
students there are, no doubt, at either end, who,
by diligent study, have made shift to comprehend
what is foreign to their ideas by nature and training—who, at least, have understood what the thing
they studied professed to be. But here is just the
difficulty. Men profess a certain thing to be *this*,
and it turns out, on examination, to be *that*—nay,
sometimes it will turn out to be neither this nor
that, only wind, sound, words without a real inner
core of meaning. Of such vain noise, inane clash-
ing together of words, there is something in every
religion, without exception. Whether there is
much or little of it in the religion of the West,
I do not pretend to know, but that there is some
I am quite certain. For instance, it is invariably
represented to us, as an essential characteristic of
the Christian religion, that it is purely monotheistic.
Christians themselves are firmly persuaded that
this is so—or rather (since persuasion connotes
some antecedent doubt) they hold to this notion
innately, from their earliest youth up, unconscious
even that there can be any question whatever
about it. But what of the bare fact, as it presents

itself—stripped of all adventitious apparel, circum-locutions, figments—to the dispassionate non-Christian inquirer? Consider, as briefly as may be, the genesis and history of this religion. But I am just off to a *concert des dames du monde*, and so I will put off what I have to say of this to my next letter.

LETTER XXV.

TOKIO, *March 22nd,* 1889.

OUR eager and confident reformers may now appraise at its true value the encouragement given to them by the foreign colony in our midst, and by European governments and their political agents. With the object of getting ourselves admitted into the comity of Western civilised nations, and of establishing the reciprocal benefits which it is supposed will flow therefrom, we have, among other things, "reformed" our judicial system—that is, we have remodelled it at all points, with submissive fidelity, so that it may present in essentials a faithful counterpart of that of Europe. So long as we were engaged in this task no praise could be too high-pitched for us; but now that we desire to turn our work to profit, to derive from it the advantages which its completion and apparent success entitle us to, we find ourselves confronted and confounded with indignant but none the less insolent remonstrances. A loud cry has gone up

136

from the foreigners here that their interests and
their security are to be sacrificed to the success of
our experiment. Why, then, did they encourage
us to undertake it? Their fears have been excited,
their pride has taken alarm, at the prospect of being
requested to submit to the jurisdiction of our
tribunals. For the sake of a fuller contact, of a
more intimate relation with Europeans, we have
overset, and at infinite pains built up anew, our code
of justice and our legal procedure. Having done
so, those who pushed us in this direction are the
first to protest against the necessary consequence
of our action.

The pretensions of these foreigners are only
equalled by their greed. No doubt those present
among us are mostly unfavourable specimens of
their respective peoples. I notice, as a matter of
fact, that prejudice and pride of race mark the
foreign residents far more strongly than the nations
from which these are drawn—that is if we may take
the views of foreign countries to be fairly reflected
in the general tone and temper of the foreign press,
The fact is, no doubt, that with the foreign colony
the present hostile feeling is due more to the
pressure of supposed personal interests than to
mere prejudice. Up to the present time these
interests have been in an especial manner safe-
guarded, not only by the presence of foreign judges
and foreign tribunals exercising jurisdiction within
our shores, but also by the absence of that com-

petition in trade which will immediately be initiated on the opening up of the interior to foreign traders who are willing to submit to native jurisdiction.

It is instructive, if somewhat disappointing, to observe how very thin is the veneer which education, quasi-philosophical views and the chatter about tolerance of judgment are able to spread upon the gross body of self-interest and personal desires. Scratch your European friend, however gently, and you come at once upon the natural man, his skin the more sensitive in that the veneer has to some extent preserved it from daily contact with rough things. So long as the changes in our political constitution, our laws, manners and customs were confined in their effects to our own people, the intelligent foreigner here present regarded these changes from the cosmopolitan, philosophical, general standpoint. His curiosity was awakened and alert as to their results, his vanity was flattered: imitation, as his people say, being the sincerest form of flattery. He himself, dwelling amid a people whose admiration of and desire for what is foreign runs upon the verge of unreason, a representative, a microcosm of the thing admired, was made much of, treated with deference, listened to with respect. The intelligent foreigner lost his head; he forgot that men, in their leading traits and master impulses, are much the same all the world over. The notion of Japanese men and women as being in general a nation of sprightly, intelligent and docile children took firm hold of his mind, and led him to misread the signs of the time. Thus, when the national pride, stimulated by the rapidity, thoroughness and success with which the programme of reform had been carried out, and flattered by the friendly and admiring attitude of the foreign powers, suddenly took offence at the proposal that Japanese laws should be partly administered by foreign judges, the intelligent foreigner was first surprised in his mistaken estimate of the Japanese character, and then alarmed in the matter of his own privileges and private interests.

On the whole the foreign press, and in general the foreign observers and critics, situated at a distance from us have followed our movements with more intelligence and with better judgment than those in our midst. I speak, of course, of the mass ; such men as ―― and ――, for instance, who to a sound judgment unite an intimate knowledge of our people, are capable of appreciations more correct than is any stranger. The infelicitous judgment and want of tact shown by the foreign colony are due, I suppose, to contact with a population which, while it has developed a civilisation of its own not widely differing from that of Europe in the feudal age, is nevertheless, in peculiarities of temperament and surface touches of character, of a type far removed from that of Europe. At bottom, however, civilised men are everywhere very much alike; and foreign critics, with judgment unbiassed by contact with our peculiarities of character, judge us by the general and natural laws to which men are everywhere subject, and thus, though often enough astray in details, are tolerable correct in the main.

Your last letter (February 7th) has just reached me. Let me say a word in reply to its concluding paragraph. You narrow too much the meaning which can rightly be attached to the word " happiness." Taking the attainment of happiness as the aim of a man's life, consider how greatly, for the vast majority of men, happiness consists in the love and good fellowship which may be made to subsist between them; and consider, further, how this mutual love and good fellowship must rest upon the services which they render to one another —in other words, upon the performance of man's duty to man. The attainment of happiness thus includes, among other things, the performance of duty. It is a mistake to exhibit these as in oppo sition to one another. Appearance of opposition there is; but that is because man, being but a foolish and purblind animal, is frequently at fault as to what his happiness consists in, frequently pursues the shadow instead of grasping the sub- stance, sacrifices permanent joy for fleeting pleasures. Only the wise know how to combine and retain the two—how occasionally to abandon a poor pleasure in order to preserve a rich joy. I am by no means surprised to hear that you are not satisfied with the philosophy of life of which you send me a sample. It is cheap and nasty, like much else now manufactured for general consumption.

LETTER XXVI.

ROME, *April 25th*, 1889.

IF we are to understand anything of the Christian religion and of how it grew to be what it now is, we must pay rather less attention than we do to the teachings of the missionaries, and rather more to those of history. And, in the first place, we shall never have the matter clearly before us until we learn at home to go back far beyond the birth of Christ, back and through the history of the ancient Hebrews, the ancestors in the flesh of the modern Jews, the spiritual forefathers of the European nations. Certain it is that within this tribe first germinated and steadily grew the idea of monotheism. The God of the Hebrews is essentially the God of the universe, the sole ruler—they themselves are his favourite sons, his "chosen people," as their sacred books put it. According to the orthodox reading of these books, and to popular tradition, the Hebrews acknowledged one universal God from the beginning; but this appears to be a pious

142

fiction, or perhaps a convenient assumption, of the theologians. There is better reason, it is said, for supposing that this idea was evolved slowly from an earlier stage of belief. It cannot, I believe, be correctly asserted that the Hebrews as a people worshipped more gods than one (except by back-sliding—which, to be sure, is in a manner to beg the question), but that they acknowledged the existence of many gods is a matter of certainty, their sacred books being constant in injunction to worship no other gods but the God of Israel, to pay no homage to the gods of other nations, their own God being jealous of such homage and apt to resent it,—the manifest idea in the minds of the writers being, not that other gods do not exist, but that they are less powerful, more unstable, less worthy of worship than the God of the Hebrews.

Gradually, and no doubt insensibly, the idea grew of a God transcending local or tribal limits. In what way or from what cause it is difficult for any one, even a close student of the subject, to say. If I dare hazard a guess, I should say that the code of morals preached to the Hebrews in the name of their God, and the system of conduct which they founded thereon, were in themselves more favourable than those of surrounding nations to the development of mental and especially moral qualities. The Hebrews, as we see them through their prophets, teachers and leaders, appear to have been at least always passionately attached to the laws and commands of their God, as leading, in the observance of them, to the predominance of the tribe and to the private success and happiness of the individuals composing it. This, it seems, was their practical experience. Their lament is, again and again, that their God forsakes them when they forsake his law. Hence the notion of something general, permanent and inviolable in the law itself, pre-eminently favourable to the conception of the monotheistic idea. What is at least sufficiently evident, from even a cursory study of the sacred writings of the Hebrews, is that in the long course of this people's history their conception of the Divine nature underwent considerable changes. The God of earlier days is distinctly a jealous, vengeful God, at times even cruel and bloodthirsty, capable of practising deceit if not of being deceived himself. He takes on himself the form of animals. He is awful indeed, for it is death to come into his visible presence; but on occasion he is to be seen by his faithful followers and by the leaders of his people, and will even speak as a friend with them. As we descend the stream of time, however, much of this is left in the background, becomes faint and then invisible. There is a growing tendency to ascribe to the Deity, as permanent attributes, the qualities of justice, mercy, absolute omniscience and omnipotence.

Nineteen hundred years ago, then, we start with

a pure form of monotheism, as the religion of the Hebrew or Jewish nation of Syria. At that time there are, in the mind and heart of the Jewish people, two distinct currents of aspiration : one, purely national, for the advent of a promised prince, to be born out of their midst (according to the prophecy of their wise men), who shall deliver them from the yoke of the alien, the hand of the oppressor ; who—in their own words—" shall make their enemies his footstool." Another, more intimate and personal, is connected with the silently growing hope of, and firmer belief in, a life beyond the grave—a belief doubtless in part fostered by weariness at the non-fulfilment of prophecy as to national emancipation, in part by the clearer perception that the just man, the follower of the divine ordinance, does by no means always meet with due measure of reward on earth. It is noticeable too that at this time the Jewish people is sunk in the meanest kind of superstition—there is a general belief in magic and witchcraft, in spells, charms, talismans and amulets, in the powers of enchantment and exorcism. Although religion is strictly monotheistic, there are wide rifts in the structure of the Church ; the people are separated into sects ; there is conflict of opinion and belief, uncertainty, turbulence of spirit. In the midst of this war of tendencies arises the grand figure of Jesus. In him there is no conflict, no uncertainty : a zeal as of fire, a sternness as of adamant, and yet a beautiful, soft serenity of soul. With a prescience almost more than human, he divines the master tendency of the age, or, plastic as the age is, he impresses his own stamp upon it. He, sole perhaps of his people, reads a new meaning into the prophecies of the past, perceives the absolute hopelessness of temporal supremacy over other nations, but perceives, too, a prospect more magnificent— a mirage, this, as of the palm grove and towered and turreted city in the wilderness, yet witness of a living reality—the prospect of the spiritual reformation of his people and the supremacy of their religion over the whole world. Strange irony of circumstances! His own people reject him, vilify him, crucify him. But, over their heads, his word goes forth to the other nations ; the breath of his spirit overturns their temples, desiccates their idols, enters into the secret chambers of men's hearts and fills them with a passionate devotion to his teaching and his memory.

What this teaching was it is now difficult, if not impossible, accurately to determine. The books which profess to embody it were, it appears, composed some considerable time after Christ's death —from one hundred to two or even three hundred years after. Competent critics also affirm that a comparison of various parts of the writings one with another supply evidence that the compilers did not always well understand the lessons of their master. But it is not the moral, so much as the theological aspect of the teaching, which has given rise to the greatest differences of opinion among Christians. It is asserted by some that in the original teaching there was no theology of the scientific kind whatever; that this was put in by the followers under the delusion that it was necessary to explain the inexplicable. Others—the great body of the orthodox—declare the theology to be the founder's own and to be binding on all who profess the Christian religion.

The sacred books and tradition laid it down as a fact that Christ declared himself to be the son of the universal God of the Hebrews, and, moreover, that in order to obtain the reward of eternal happiness, his followers must not only conform to his moral teaching, but believe in his divine origin. This was the corner-stone of the foundation on which the subsequent fabric of dogma was upbuilt. It was accepted that Christ was a God, or God. But it was known from the sacred writings, and from tradition, that he certainly had a reputed human father and mother, and brothers too. Here was a difficulty. Evidently the reputed parents of a God could not be ordinary persons. The first step taken was to declare the mother (Mary) to have borne Jesus, in the human sense, as a virgin. The inexorable process of logic next led to the establishing of some kind of connection between the universal God of the Hebrews, the father of Christ, and the Virgin his mother. At this point another God comes into the field of belief: the Holy Ghost. It is not clear whence this God derives his origin. He must have existed from all time, of course, but previously to these events had been unknown to people. In general he appears in the light of a divine messenger, sometimes between the Father and the Son, sometimes between the Son and his followers. In the case of the birth of Christ he appears as a messenger from the Father to the Virgin— Jesus is said to be conceived by him: a miraculous birth, on which, together with the miracles performed by Jesus during his ministry, rests the credibility of the whole body of Christian dogma.

So far, then, there is a distinct falling away from the monotheistic idea. According to the sacred writings there are three Gods, and in this notion ignorant and untheological persons would doubtless willingly have rested. But the theologians and rulers of the Church, mindful of the Hebrew origin of their religion, mindful also of the essentially monotheistic character of the Hebrew religion, were evidently much exercised to reconcile apparently hostile ideas, and to combat the natural tendency to put a polytheistic complexion on what they considered was a monotheistic religion. From this arose a vast and ever-increasing mass of metaphysical disquisition on the nature of the Deity, the Church finally accepting the incomprehensible proposition that the three Gods are one and at the same time three. I had a most interesting conversation on this point with a very intelligent French priest here, one of the order of Jesuits ; but of this more in my next letter.

LETTER XXVII.

TOKIO, *April 6th*, 1889.

YOU must remember the student riots which took place in the early part of 1888, when those young men were good enough to afford the Government the benefit of their experienced advice as to needful measures of reform, and the intimidation and violence to which they resorted—promptly put down though they were—as a means of calling attention to their views. It was then that I first became seriously troubled as to the dangers and difficulties which certainly await us along our path of reform. For many years the conservatism and distrust of change which are natural to old age have been making their influence more and more felt with me, but until this affair of the students I had only realised in an abstract way the extreme danger which follows when the order of a nation's life is thrown open to undisciplined thought and rash discussion. These young men are all for reasoning instead of acquiring knowledge, for logic in the place of experience, for abstract ideas at the expense of concrete facts. If the mechanism of the nation's life is at variance with their ideas, so much the worse, say they, for the mechanism—we must break it up and construct anew. *They* will take charge of that, and doubtless the materials will come to hand of their own accord.

The dangers which thus trouble me are of very old standing—as old as thought itself. Every nation has suffered them, but, with a little firmness and saving common sense (where the majority has been thus favoured), has contrived to escape shipwreck. A worse danger than these, however, is apparent to me in these days: not that which springs from reckless comparisons between various systems of morals and codes of conduct, but from the too prevalent disposition to treat these as interesting general problems rather than as important practical ones, and even to hint the question as to whether any system of morals is of permanently binding force. To let drop careless words and phrases on such matters is not unlike emptying the burning ashes of your pipe in the immediate vicinity of a powder barrel.

There is growing in our midst a large, a much too large and easy-going tolerance in matters of conduct and in the free expression of opinion; a tendency to look upon moral laws as mere conventional rules, which may at pleasure be altered or amended according to circumstances, hence to conclude that a rigid code of conduct is an absurdity; from which conclusion an easy step takes the individual to the doctrine that he may permit himself to say and do anything which his fellows will not forcibly prevent him from saying and doing, and, further, that they will usually be wrong in thus hindering him. "There is no such thing as morality in the abstract" is the kind of lesson which just now I hear very glibly taught by advanced persons among us. That is true enough, though perhaps not quite in the sense intended by the teacher. Morality in the abstract is for man in the abstract, with whom, outside of books, we have nothing to do. If by "abstract" is meant "absolute," the sentence gains in meaning, but it conveys at best but a half truth, barren in its application to the affairs of life. At every moment of a man's life there must be an absolutely "rightest" thing for him to do; he may not be able or willing to do it, but that does not alter the fact. A code of morals, to be absolute, must take into account every circumstance in which a man may find himself. To such completeness no code attains, but it is absolute so far as it applies. You may extend the argument (which, in truth, is more or less verbal) from a man to a community of men, from the community to the nation, from the nation to the race, and so on to men in general : the code of morals may be said to remain absolute while becoming more and more restricted in its application as the area widens, as the circumstances become more complex, and as the conditions of men's lives become more disparate.

The increased and rapidly increasing means of communication between all parts of the world, and the swift dissemination of knowledge as to the modes of thought and the habits of life of various peoples, must in the end prove beneficial to the human race, by the gradual elimination of the useless and the preservation of the useful.; but in the meantime the effect of all this is to unsettle men's minds, to introduce chaos into the order of ideas. Nowhere is this more noticeable than in the domain of morals and religion. It is in the nature of man to pass from one extreme to another. Once shake his belief that the order in which he lives is not absolute, and his imagination soon runs riot. From the conviction that his own system of morality and code of conduct should be of universal application, he passes to the opinion that nothing in any system or code is everywhere applicable. At this point morality, in his eyes, assumes the character of convention, devoid of any inherent truth or falseness.

A moral idea is not true or false in itself, but only in its general application to life. An edible is not sweet or bitter in itself, but only in relation to the palate. The truth or untruth of a moral idea is as absolute as the sweetness or bitterness of an edible—no more and no less. There are palates—we call them diseased—which fail to discern between the two, which will even pronounce sweet to be bitter and bitter sweet.   Reasoning on some such analogy as this, the advanced young person in our midst comes down on us with the proposition that moral precepts are to be pronounced true or false precisely as things are pronounced sweet or bitter, that is, according to the prevalent conviction of the majority.   I admire the advanced young person's hardihood in analogy more, much more, than his judgment in practical matters.   To compare an appeal to reason with an appeal to sensation, and thence to make a parallel deduction with the object of applying it to the conduct of life, is a perilously summary intellectual proceeding. Our sensations never, or very rarely, deceive us ; they are the foundation on which rests all our knowledge, on which reason builds, well or badly ; we are bound to trust them, or the world would become a chaos to us.   Our reason, on the other hand, is frequently at fault, the judgment of one generation is frequently reversed by that of its successor.   A moral precept is right or wrong according to whether its observance makes or makes not for the well-being of the human race as a whole ; but an entire generation of men or suc-cessive generations may easily be at fault in such a matter, for, in fine, it is experience and reason together which decide.   Thus, when the advanced young person comes down on us with his proposi-tion that moral precepts are right or wrong accord-

ing to the prevalent opinion of the majority, he
is either mistaken in his view or meaningless in
his language : mistaken, if by right or wrong he
understands that which makes or not for well-being;
meaningless, if he merely defines prevalent opinion
as *ipso facto* right opinion, for in that case he strips
right and wrong of the meaning which men attach
to them.

LETTER XXVIII.

TOKIWARA TO YASHIRI.

ROME, *April* 16*th*, 1889.

IN my last letter, I think I said something of a conversation I had with a Jesuit father on one of the essential dogmas of the Christian religion : the Trinity in Unity, and Unity in Trinity. The good priest, an amiable and intelligent man, was benignly surprised, and, I suspect, secretly amused, that a foreigner from idolatrous lands should look upon his religion as one of the many forms of polytheism. So far as I can trust myself to have understood him, it appears that the orthodox Christian belief is not in three Gods, but in one. The apparent three Gods are really three distinct manifestations of the same being. He gave me an ingenious illustration of his meaning, drawn from the science of chemistry. If you introduce a diamond between the two carbon points of a powerful electric arc light, so that the current passes through the diamond, it is turned into a piece of pure carbon without admixture of any other element, such as the oxygen or nitrogen of the air. The substance is the same, although it appears under two different forms : diamond and carbon. So, too, the chemical element sulphur is met with in three distinct modifications : always precisely the same substance, but coming under cognisance of our senses in three distinct manners. I was delighted with this, to me, novel way of putting the matter. "Take this diamond," said the good father (giving me, not a gem, but an illustration) "and this carbon. We are told they are made of the same elemental substance : carbon. But, with equal truth, we might be told : diamond. Diamond is carbon with its molecules in one order of aggregation. Carbon is diamond with *its* molecules in another order of aggregation. Is the molecule carbon or diamond? The elemental molecule is the same in both. *We* see two manifestations of the same substance—the latter a profound mystery to us." He took snuff with emotion, not unimpressive to me.

On reflection, however, I found I had not greatly advanced towards a satisfactory understanding of this difficult matter. The Christian Deity is not sometimes this, sometimes that, and sometimes the other, but always and at the same time one and three. The most strenuous exercise of good will and imagination, however, fails to bring home to me how a substance can at the same time be diamond and carbon. Sulphur under three different modifications may be reduced to one form, but then it could not simultaneously be in three forms.

Enough, enough, this road surely leads to madness.
In the course of further conversation with others,
it became apparent to me that when wise people
are driven into a corner over these matters,
they admit the propositions to be not humanly explicable, and therefore to be frankly accepted as
mysteries. There is much virtue in the "therefore." Whatsoever the ultra-wise, the metaphy-
sicians, the theologians, may make of such matters,
it is indubitable that the common run of mortals,
judging by myself, have little or no faculty for
drawing subtle distinctions between substance,
essence, modes, attributes and the rest of it. They
were told that three Gods are one, and, some
under compulsion of reverence for their teachers,
others under fear of damnation for disbelief, accepted the proposition simply as a matter of faith
too mysterious for comprehension. But the most
honest, unfeigned assent to mysteries, how excellent soever may sometimes be its effect on conduct,
scarcely tends to improve the understanding. The
initial movement once given, the simple but grand
idea of one all-knowing, all-powerful, self-sufficient
God once tampered with, there followed gradually
all that we now see. First the virgin mother was
raised to the position of Queen of Heaven. In
Roman Catholic prints I think I have seen her
seated at the left hand of God, Jesus Christ being
on the right hand, the Holy Ghost absent or
vaguely symbolised. Then, with the fatal facility

of the polytheistic idea, men who had distinguished themselves by dying for the Christian faith, or by living lives of superior sanctity, were raised to the position of lesser gods, invoked under the name of saints. These things were done naturally, inevitably, by the simple religious souls and the practical pious people; and as fast as they were done the metaphysical theologians had to spin the cobwebs which enmeshed nascent reasoning wherever and whenever it fluttered forth on callow wing.

The duties of the Christian priesthood resemble those of other religious ministrants. They conduct the religious services, set an example of life and conduct to their flocks, expound the Scriptures and interpret the dogmas of the faith. In the Roman Catholic Church the true interpretation of dogma is held to reside in the Church as a body. The voice of the Church on a question of dogma is spoken through its head, the Pope, who, on such occasions, is believed to be divinely inspired and therefore infallible in his decision. This is a great comfort to the devout Roman Catholic, for he is thus spared the necessity of reflection and the danger of wrong decision. He believes what he is told to believe. And this surely is very logical, the dogmas to be received being avowedly mysteries. But there seems to be a slight rift in the logic at another point. The position of the individual Roman Catholic is comprehensible; but that of the Church as a body is perplexing. Its claim is that, through its head, it interprets the divine mysteries to the body of the faithful. But is it not in the essence of a mystery that it is incomprehensible and inexplicable ? Thus the Church interprets the incomprehensible in such a manner that it becomes explained while remaining mysterious ; or perhaps what it does is to explain that the mysterious is the incomprehensible ; this indeed would be an infallible decision, though it would scarcely seem to require any more divine inspiration than that of common sense. But this makes another road to madness ; indeed, I may remark incidentally that they have a saying in England that, next to love, religion has driven more persons crazy than any other matter whatsoever.

LETTER XXIX.

YASHIRI TO TOKIWARA.

TOKIO, *April* 19*th*, 1889.

You will forgive an old man, distressed by the anarchy of thought and the confusion of change which surround him, these somewhat prosy and hortatory letters. I feel the want to review exactly, and to make quite plain to myself and to you, the standpoint which I occupy, as well as to explain why it is that so much which is going on here is of a nature which I can neither approve nor reconcile myself to. I feel out of sympathy with, and in much even opposed to, the advanced young person of these latter days—nowhere more so than in the conception of the relations which permanently bind men together: relations which have grown to be what they are in the long lapse of centuries, and which should be handled discreetly and in a reverent spirit, not buffeted and dragged hither and thither in sportive or lawless fashion.

Whatever may be the ultimate benefit to be reaped from the right comprehension of the modern theory of Evolution, I perceive that its ready acceptance and fortuitous application by the advanced young person is not without distinct menace of danger to the national well-being. In every department with which statesmanship is concerned the tendency of the advanced young person is to legislate in view, not of what his countrymen are, but of what he thinks they are likely to, or ought to, become. Were everybody agreed, were even a considerable number of the intelligent and educated agreed, as to what *is* the true course of progress, this tendency of the advanced young person should meet with encouragement; but the very plain evidence of these days is that never before have there existed ideals of progress so many and so diverse. But the advanced young person is scientific or nothing, and he therefore very justly points out that discussion about true progress is not likely to help us greatly, that the course of development is necessary: the resultant of what has gone before, the effect of pre-existing causes. But, as among these causes—which are to bring about the necessary effect—are included our own endeavours and exertions, the contribution from science for our guidance is not very helpful, either to the individual in his private affairs or to the statesman in the framing and safeguarding of laws and institutions. And then, our own endeavours and exertions, these also are effects of predisposing causes; why, then, trouble ourselves as to what these endeavours and exertions shall be

. . . and so on in endless perplexity—so that, to escape therefrom, we are ever driven to assume a principle of free initiative in man, as modifying the otherwise necessary result of antecedent causes.

Legislation which is ambitious and looks very far ahead, labours under the disadvantage of never being exactly fit either for the present or for the future. The law-maker, and, for that matter, all of us, are under compulsion to represent to ourselves the path of progress, or the line of evolution, as proceeding continuously in the direction to which points our notion of progress or evolution at the time. But every fresh increment of knowledge gained as we go on tends to modify our acquired conception of the path's direction. The constitution of our minds predisposes us to figure progress to ourselves as a right line—the resultant of previous experiences ; perhaps, bearing in mind what the future shrouds of experience for us, we should be nearer the mark in using for symbol an infinite curve.

Especially am I moved to dissatisfaction and to contention—profitless, I fear—with the advanced young person, because of his airy statement that morality is nothing but convention. It disquiets me to reflect how commonly abuse of words leads to abuse of things. Conventions I understand to be agreements as to what I may call the surface conduct of life, agreements mostly informal, and which may obviously be cancelled or replaced by others of a like nature without greatly affecting the relations of men to one another in the important affairs of life. If the advanced young person really means that moral laws are precisely the same as conventions, I can only suppose that he has withdrawn himself to so great a distance from real men and women that distinctions quite plain to us have become imperceptible to him. If his meaning is that it is impossible accurately to draw a line between moral laws and conventions, I agree with him ; but neither is it possible accurately to draw a line between riches and poverty, yet the distinction between these is very real and very useful, although in this case but one of degree merely, whereas in the other it is well-nigh a distinction of kind. True, by grouping all that morality even remotely connotes under the term convention, we simplify ideas for abstract discussion and more readily reach general conclusions, but the conclusions thus reached are more than ever difficult of application to the facts of life.

It is not that I grudge the advanced young person the rather arid pleasure of logic-chopping, but I object to the consequences which are likely to follow from the dissemination of his theories. It is but seldom that moral and intellectual progress run together on all fours. Progress in intellect proceeds by the way of inquiry, in morality by the way of discipline and practice. Free inquiry into moral ideas is hostile to their stability, though not perhaps to their final permanence ; it acts on them as a temporary dissolvent. The dispassionate and clear-minded student may perceive that systems of morals have been gradually built up upon the necessities of life in common ; that codes of conduct, like trees, however much they may differ in detail, grow up in much the same way everywhere, in accordance with the general laws of growth. But from the moment the average individual accepts this as a fact, the moral law under which he lives, no longer held as an immediate divine and imperative ordinance, will lose force and efficacy. He will infallibly begin to question its claim to bind him personally. He will, whenever he finds it convenient, consider a moral obligation as a convention to be admitted only if inevitable. In fine, the spirit of opportunism will supplant that of duty as the guide of conduct. A mere abuse of words will lead of itself to an abuse of things : a man may easily be too heedful of convention, but scarcely of morality.

LETTER XXX.

ROME, *April* 30*th*, 1889.

ADMITTING that we should do well to foster the Christian religion in Japan—a point which, as you perceive, I have forborne to discuss, not feeling equal to the task—the matter next in importance is : which of the Christian religions? Neither shall I discuss this, but merely tell you, from my coign of vantage here, how their differences, their separate advantages and disadvantages, strike me. We need scarcely consider the claims of the Greek Church to our attention. It is not a distinctly proselytising sect, and, so far as I know, has no adherents at home. It differs but little in doctrine and ritual from the Church of Rome ; its principal offence in the eyes of the latter lying in its rejection of the papal authority. The break between the two is of old standing; it occurred more than seven hundred years ago. At the bottom of it was the rivalry, both political and religious, between the eastern and western capitals of the Roman empire. The pretext for separation was afforded by some trivial dispute concerning the use of images in the temples and in the ceremonial of worship. The breach widened, the disputants called one another by opprobrious names—idolaters and iconoclasts. The latter cast off their nominal allegiance to the Pope.

The rupture between Roman Catholics and Protestants was of a totally different character, and, in its inception at least, due to more reputable motives. It is alleged by the Protestants, and, I believe admitted by the fair-minded and well-informed among their opponents, that in the sixteenth century of the Christian era the discipline and morals of the Church, especially among the higher ecclesiastics, left much to be desired. A simple German monk, one Luther, went to Rome filled with pious enthusiasm and veneration, and stayed there just long enough to learn how to empty his bosom of these very misplaced sentiments, and to refill it with others of a different kind. When he got home again to his own country, he raised the standard of religious revolt against certain abuses of the power of Rome, and assailed the scandalous life of some of the high prelates. He found a party ready to support him, for political as well as religious reasons. The strife was embittered by the introduction of dissent on points of doctrine. For a hundred years Western Europe was one vast battle-field for the contending parties, victory now inclining one way and now the other. Finally, Rome retained the allegiance of the Latin races and lost

that of the others.   Long before the close of the
contest Rome was reformed in discipline and
conduct, but on either side passions were far too
excited, minds much too envenomed, to admit of a
reconciliation.   The Roman Catholics branded the
reformers as heretics and anarchists in religion;
the Protestants on their side looked on their
opponents as idolaters, the more virulent among
them applying to the Popes of Rome the most
scandalous and disgusting epithets.

But it is not my purpose to enter at any length
into the causes and history of these dissensions,
nor to examine the differences of dogma between
the two sects.   All I need remark as to this is—
what doubtless you already know—that the Protestants do not make gods of their Saints, nor
assign to the Virgin Mary the same place or power
as do the Roman Catholics.   For us, the important
practical point to consider is the difference of
religious spirit which animates these two great
sects.   We should not, I think, go very wide astray
in saying that the dominant characteristic of the
true Roman Catholic is respect for authority and
a sense of the value of discipline, while that which
especially marks the Protestant is his possession of
the safeguard against abject superstition which lies
in his assertion of the right of private judgment in ·
religion.   If we travel from end to end, from the
extreme limit of one sect to that of the other, we
pass from spiritual despotism to spiritual anarchy.

I do not mean by the latter free-thought, but anarchy in dogma and ritual, especially ritual.   Both extremes lead to free-thought, one by the road of revolt against absolutism, the other by the easy path of licence in opinion.   The tendency of Protestantism to anarchy in religion was clearly foreseen and predicted by the great champion of Roman Catholicism in the seventeenth century of the Christian era : the French bishop (chief bonze) Bossuet.

So far as the more forward nations of Europe have a vital religion, that religion is undoubtedly the Protestant one.   Many individual Protestants point to it as having made the Protestant nations that which they now are.   I can scarcely believe that to be so.   How far should we find an idea of that kind borne out at our end of the world ? Take the Chinese and ourselves, for instance.   The Chinese are as essentially conservative as we are progressive.   Yet an immense part of our spiritual inheritance is derived, either directly or indirectly, from China.   In religion, Buddhism has permeated the great mass of our people, partly by direct adoption, partly by a process of grafting on the more ancient Kami-worship.   Our Samurai and, in general, the upper classes are, like those of China, followers of Confucius.   Yet how essentially different is the spirit which informs the two nations !   I cannot believe that their religion has had any but a quite secondary and indirect influence on the development of the Protestant nations. That development has in the main been due, I take it, to an inborn spirit of initiative and enterprise, and to an inherent capacity for self-government. Such a spirit was bound to be captivated by, and was in fact allied to, the spirit which animates the Protestant religion.

But it must be admitted that, although the adoption of Protestantism was due to a certain bias or tendency of mind in the Teutonic nations, yet this religion has in turn reacted on the general disposition of the peoples which adopted it. Every religion which influences conduct by fixing men's minds on an ideal future life is, in theory, a faulty religion. And it is faulty exactly in the proportion in which the scheme of conduct which it inculcates (with a view to the future life), departs from the conduct which in actual life makes for progress and happiness. Every religion which has laid firm hold on great masses of men, and kept its hold, has been enabled to do so because its founder and his followers have had a clear insight into the minds and hearts of men, have correctly judged what kind of conduct really makes for the happiness and progress of men. And, in this connection, it is well worthy of remark that the three great religions, which, if we exclude the purely savage races, rule among them the whole world, prescribe codes of conduct which do not in any essential feature differ from one another. The truth is that the

vast majority of men do not compass their well-
being by dreaming about what may be, but by
paying attention to what is.   Put such a proposition
in a general way to a sensible Christian, and he
will surely agree with you.   Ask him to apply it
to his view of religion, and he will recoil from it,
although the whole tenor of his life plainly proves
that the moving power in it is the actual and present,
that it is influenced only remotely and vaguely by
the possible and future.   And, indeed, the history
of the development of Christianity affords in itself
the best evidence of the revolt of a healthy religion
from the tyranny of a visionary ideal.   Surely, if
this life were but a momentary preparation for
eternity, if conduct had nothing to do with happiness on this earth, if, by the side of a giant
expectation, earthly affairs and affections sank into
absolute insignificance, what could be more natural,
more logical, than the tendency of mediæval
Christianity? What mattered learning, art, science,
industry? what mattered anything save adoration,
the subjugation of the flesh as preparation for the
life of the spirit, and charity because commanded
by the founder?   But Christianity itself gave the
lie to this ideal—only in its extreme form, however :
it retained as much of the ideal as could be made
to fit in with practical needs and rational desires.

Protestantism, too, came in the course of time
to be touched with the same spirit of revolt against
making this earth in practice, as well as in theory,

a mere waiting-room to eternity. The belief in the merit of a monastic life, as that best fitted to reach heaven by, suffered a total eclipse—wherein Protestants showed sound common sense in the application of ideals to life, and characteristic contempt for logic in religion. "Why so?" inquired one of them, with whom I was conversing on the subject. "It is surely a nobler kind of life to brave and withstand the temptations of the world than to shut oneself up out of their reach." I inquired of him whether he believed the prayers of his Church, especially that known as the "Lord's Prayer," to be the inspiration of Divine wisdom. "Certainly," he replied. "Then," I said, "if the life you set down as the less noble were so in God's sight, would not your prayer be 'give us strength to withstand temptation' rather than 'lead us not into temptation'? and how can a man better help himself—that God may help him—than by withdrawing as far as possible from the temptations of the world?" He was speechless, though he babbled on for a quarter of an hour.

In discountenancing celibacy of the priesthood, too, Protestants showed the same vigorous common sense, as also in making the practice of religious ceremonial less a part of their daily lives than is the case with the Roman Catholics. With Protestants in general, even the devout ones, it is always business first, and other matters, religion included, afterwards. This is perhaps why they have on the whole gone on more smoothly and comfortably than their brethren of the older form of faith ; the minding of business immediately at hand being more sensible and profitable than that of business which is far away in the future, and which, indeed, cannot properly be minded at all.

On the whole, then, since the political philosophers declare that we must have a religion, and that no religion can at present be at all helpful with the masses which is not dogmatic, I should be inclined, if Christianity it is to be, to recommend it under the Protestant form, notwithstanding the far greater similarity in ritual between Buddhism and Roman Catholicism, which would certainly help the introduction and dissemination of the latter. But I am thinking of the more lasting effects. Protestantism withdraws the attention of people less urgently from the conduct of their own affairs and those of the nation. It leaves them less under a spirit of blind obedience to authority, and therefore more watchful and critical of government. It is hostile to the dominance of a priestly caste, which, of all tyrannies, is perhaps the most difficult to shake off. And, lastly, if it be possible ever to construct a religion which shall be free from dogma concerning the unknowable, the Protestant religion, by its natural tendency to protest and dissent, rather than to abide in affirmation, will afford us the easiest path to that very desirable end.

LETTER XXXI.

YASHIRI TO TOKIWARA.

TOKIO, *May 5th*, 1889.

FROM what filters to us over here of the current
literature of Europe, I gather that one of the
principal things which preoccupy statesmen—I
speak not of politicians—and vex the souls of
philosophers and reformers, is the inequitable
distribution of wealth in their respective countries.
The tendency, so it would seem, is for the rich to
grow richer and the poor poorer. But I ask
myself whether this is really the case, whether
the publicity, which nowadays attends all things
and makes every man's doings the concern of his
neighbour, is not responsible for this assertion;
responsible, that is, through the carelessness of the
casual onlooker, who perhaps fails to make due
allowance for the fact—as I take it to be—that the
difference between the rich and the poor is at the
present time thrown into stronger and more general
relief than heretofore : publicity painting the contrast in more glaring colours.

I ask myself this because I notice that whenever

the dissatisfied reformer lifts up his voice in plain-
tive or indignant howl, and persists therein long
enough to awaken general attention, some quiet
person usually comes to the front, armed with
apparently unassailable facts and figures, to prove
the reverse; or, if not altogether the reverse, at
least that the poor are certainly not getting poorer,
but are now better off than they have ever been
before.

Always and steadily keeping in view that, be it
for good or ill, we are entering upon the path
which the nations of the West have trodden down
for us, questions such as these attract my attention,
excite my hopes and fears for the future. From
this distant corner of the earth my suspicion goes
forth to you—for confirmation or otherwise—that
possibly the explanation of such a conflict of
opinion lies in this : that the persons concerned to
take a just view are unable so to do from sheer
proximity to the object under scrutiny, cannot get
a bird's-eye view of its general form and complexion.
Of this vast and complex Industrial System—
growing vaster and more complex every day—an
observer will observe well here, another observer
well there, but, as to the whole, observation may
be defective. Naturally, I speak without intimate
knowledge of the subject, as a mere distant beholder of what is in process, and with the object
rather of directing your attention thereto than of
propounding a solution. Still, I will say what

I think, were it only to lead you to think what you shall say.

It seems to me, then, that the development of the industrial system in Europe is just such, as to give rise to the apparently unconsidered opinion that the rich are growing richer and the poor poorer, that the distribution of wealth is day by day becoming more inequitable. For, unquestionably, if the line of demarcation, of local separation between rich and poor, is becoming more trenchant and therefore more observed, if the poor are found to be dwelling more in masses, more separated from the rich, superficial observers will be found to declare that inequity in distribution of wealth is on the increase, that the rich are growing richer and the poor poorer. Yet possibly the case is quite otherwise. That such a constitution of society may be resting upon something rotten or dangerous is very likely, but the useful thing to do would be to point to the real danger, not to invent imaginary ones, the parading of which must distract attention from the real.

I am going on a mere assumption, of course. I am supposing it to be actually the case that the development of industry is being accompanied by an increased herding together of the poor and a gathering of the rich into closer intimacy with one another. Is my assumption justified by the facts? —that is what I should much like you to inquire into. By the " poor," of course, I understand the working class in general. To ascertain the facts is perhaps a harder matter than I imagine, but I shall be surprised if you tell me they are not very patent, very observable to the most ordinary capacity for seeing. For consider what has been the steady tendency of industrial enterprise, visible even over here, during these last decades: agglomeration of small businesses into large ones, of small factories into large factories, of retail shops into monster stores, of individual traders into co-operative societies; distinction and separation between those who direct, who work with their brains, and those who are directed, who work with their hands. A hundred years ago, so far as I can gather from my reading, the master in any trade or craft in Europe was both head and hand worker; with him were associated some few assistants, who lived either with him or near him, and who, at any rate, must have been in daily personal and intimate contact with him. The great leaders of industry and employers of labour, the great masses of workers all at work in one spot and under one direction, were then non-extant, undreamed of. In these days, a factory master who employs five hundred or a thousand hands clearly cannot be on intimate terms with them all; his personal connection with them must be perfunctory, more or less nominal. Moreover, in any large industrial district it must be a consequence of the work to be done and of the manner of doing it that the

12

labourers and artisans herd together, and it must follow as surely that such districts will be un-attractive to, and hence unfrequented by the rich. I understand that in the mining counties of England the miners form communities, and even towns, which consist almost exclusively of the miners themselves and the purveyors of their necessaries, and of their pleasures, if such they have.   In the large cities I hear that whole quarters are being gradually pulled down and rebuilt in square miles of industrial dwellings, not only differing in charac-ter, but widely sundered in position, from those of the rich.   It is an inevitable inference from all this that there is being traced, between rich and poor, a line of demarcation more marked than hitherto, more evident to the general gaze.

When classes are thus sundered, separation tends to become identified with opposition ; the notion of opposed class-interests gains in definiteness and strength, there is a loss of the common fellow-feeling of man for man.   Habitual contact between men, however different their stations, breeds sympathy ; loss of contact leads to indifference.   It is true that at all times and places the rich live by the labour of the poor, and the poor partly by the expenditure of the rich ; but when the organisation of society is patriarchal or feudal, or society itself still touched with the patriarchal or feudal senti-ment, this relation between rich and poor is softened, glossed over, made more supportable by the general relations which subsist between them, and which imply some modicum of care and protection on the one part, of deference and obedience on the other. As it appears to me now, at this time, the relation between the two is merely commercial. The rich man says in effect to the poor, and the poor man to the rich : " Let each one of us mind his own business, and, with as little haggling and delay as may be, exchange money for labour, and labour for money; beyond this traffic between us there is nothing." That such an attitude of class towards class can be enduring, can be even endurable, is possible, but does not seem likely. It is not open to predict with wisdom what the era of industrialism will make of man's condition and circumstances, but of one thing we may be well assured : that his nature will remain what it now is and has been in the past. Suspicion, distrust, envy, jealousy, are embers which smoulder ever in men's hearts, and which a faint breath of discontent will fan forth into flames of destruction. In a society so constituted that the rich live apart from and unrespected by the poor, that the poor exist unwatched and uncared for by the rich, there must needs be peril. More so than ever in this the industrial era, where the ideal of society is— mark it well—the production and accumulation of wealth before all things, as leading to all things. Given such an ideal, together with such a juxta- position of classes, what wonder if poverty become synonymous with hell, riches with elysium? I cannot picture to myself a more unstable condition of things, one less likely to be permanent, because supremely unsatisfying to the vast mass of human beings, whose fate it must be to toil, to live in poverty, in this hell of their minds' making.

For some reasons I am inclined to think that the evils which the industrial system bears in its train may come to us modified and tempered, because of certain peculiarities which markedly differentiate us from the Western nations. But this letter is already long enough, and I shall do well to take a little more time, from what the gods may yet allow me, to reflect at ease on the matter. More of this in my next letter.

LETTER XXXII.

LONDON, *May 15th*, 1889.

BACK in London again, and not a word to you
about Rome! What should I say of Rome?
This only, that during the greater part of my
sojourn there I lay as if a-dreaming. A glittering
but confused phantasmagoria of the past unrolled
itself unceasingly before me ; but much as I might
try—vainly, as in a dream—I could make out no
clear pictures, so different—beyond the power of
imagination—must this past have been from that
to which the history of our own land has attuned
our thoughts. The ruined Forum, and its countless
associations, the palace of the Cæsars, the Capitol,
the Colosseum, the columns, the arches, the spectral
pageants: processions, ovations, triumphs, the echoes
of acclaim from the lion-throated multitude, the
cackling of the geese, the roar of the wild beasts,
the fold of the toga, the rose-crowned reclining
forms of the banquet-hall, the laurel wreath and
the chaplet of gems—all swam before me in glorious
disorder, reckless of time, sequence and association.

Back in London once more—in England, the

land of business—so, to business again. I want to hark back for the moment to what is at present immeasurably the most important point on which the attention of our leading men should fix itself: the growth of a middle or distributive class in the western parts of Europe, and all which this growth and not altogether gracious presence means now and foreshadows for the future. I perceive two very distinct features about a society which includes such a class. The first is what is called "credit," elusive, impalpable, an airy fabric of the mind, but none the less real on that account; the second is the manipulator of credit—the capitalist, or rather the capitalist and the banker, for between the two credit is organised and made subservient to industry. Do you know what is a capitalist? Perhaps you may recollect a discussion, which some of us younger men had at your house last year, as to the nature of capital, when, on referring to a standard European text-book on political economy, it was made plain that capital is that portion of the produced wealth of a nation which is especially set apart and used for the reproduction of wealth : that part, as it were, of the rice crops which is not consumed but set apart for the sower. A capitalist, then, I said to myself, must be one who owns this kind of wealth and turns it to account in producing more : a kind of sower who casts his seed, not into the soil, but into the productive hands of the people. But here the analogy ceases, for the capitalist himself by no means reaps the whole crop. In the present industrial stage of such a country as this it may be said without paradox that capitalists, as a body, have really made away with their capital, turned it over to the people, and, in the place of it, hold promises of repayment in money value, together with supplementary promises of interest or of profits. Thus it seems that a capitalist is essentially a capitalist when he ceases to own actual capital. At a former time, when he or, say, his father held actual capital, he (or his father) was, oddly enough, probably not a capitalist, but a merchant, manufacturer, or what not. The distinction may seem to you wire-drawn, over-subtle; but, as I go on, you will perceive that it has an important application. A young and rising member of the legislature, to whom I was speaking of these matters, remonstrated with me for making, as he averred, distinctions so theoretical. " Surely," he said, "a capitalist is rightly named; for, although he may not be in possession of actual capital, he can at any moment re-enter into possession by selling the promises on paper which he holds." This, of course, I was ready enough to admit; but I could point out with truth that if one, or six, or six-score capitalists could at any moment re-enter into possession of actual capital, capitalists as a body certainly could not, for the simple reason that in attempting to do so they would bring about a general bankruptcy. If we look at the matter without prejudice of a European commercial education, we shall see that not only have the capitalists, as a body, relinquished their capital for the sake of prospective profits and annuities, but that, were they to attempt to lay hands on it again, it would in a manner melt beneath the touch, inasmuch as the very gesture would bring industry and commerce to a standstill.   In truth, what are called in England the capitalists are naught else than the creditors of the nation—I do not mean the holders of national debt stock, for these are merely possessors of a claim to perennial annuities, not to principal—I mean all those whose property (as a body) really consists in claims on the present and future productive capacity of the people.

In fact, what a capitalist really owns is nothing else than credit, or debt, which is the same thing as credit, looked at from the opposite point of view. In a highly civilised nation, where contracts are not only strictly enforced by law, but voluntarily complied with from a sense of commercial honour, such credits are looked upon as being as good as, and more convenient than, the sums of money which they represent.   And here the bankers step in, and, with prestidigital ease, commence to circulate this credit, and, like skilful conjurers, from every portion of it to make ten other portions. People, even in England, have a hazy notion that bankers take charge of their money, keep a portion of it in the bank till, and lend out the remainder at interest. But their operations, as explained to me by an expert, are more grandiose than this. Some part of the money they no doubt lend, another part they keep for meeting daily calls, but there is a third part which serves them as a means greatly to extend their business. On a cash basis of a hundred *yen* they will lend a thousand, by actually creating credits on their books for commercial men in whom they have confidence—the profit they derive being from the interest charged on these loans of credit. I fancy you will now easily enough see how it is that these nations are afflicted now and again with the commercial crises and panics of which we hear, without well understanding what they mean. They must arise from two different though allied causes. First when, from danger of war, sedition, subversive legislation, or any like matter, the more timorous capitalists ·endeavour to re-enter into possession of their capital or its money value, or refuse to lend what small portion of it may be in their hands. Secondly, when some large bank or commercial house fails, or is reported to be in difficulties : in this case the affiliation which is known to exist between the defaulting or shaky establishment and others (to which it probably owes money) causes what is termed here "a run" to be made on both; people hurry there in order to get their credits turned into cash ; but as there is an immense amount more credit than cash, this cannot be done: thus is wrought a fresh risk of failure, and it is not difficult to see that the more frightened people become the worse grow the consequences.

This subject, I admit, is a very dull one; I have therefore only touched on the salient points of it, but I believe its clear comprehension to be of the utmost importance for us. I do not, of course, profess to understand it in detail myself: no doubt there are some who do understand it thoroughly, but I have not been fortunate enough to meet them, or one of them. I have looked through several learned books on the subject of credit with small profit to myself, seeing that they disagree on most essential points. If Europeans could be induced to give us some good lessons on this invention of their own, instead of chattering to us about art, we should have reason to be grateful to them.

Although capitalists and bankers are not in themselves particularly interesting persons, yet the origin of the rise and establishment of the modern plutocracy is worthy of notice. In order to understand this it is necessary to look back some two hundred years. About this time, in England, the development of industries and the extension of trade had already set foot upon the prosperous path which has since led them so fair and far. The nucleus of the present middle class was already in existence, and there was also a fair amount of amassed wealth in the country. It occurred to some acute persons about this time that the increasing difficulty of obtaining supplies for the prosecution of wars and other useful enterprises might be obviated by borrowing, on the credit of the Government, from this tempting provision in the hands of rich citizens.   The king, his ministers, and, in general, the official class were delighted with the simplicity of the proposal, with the convenience of a system which promised to save them from the odium and danger attached to the practice of wringing piecemeal, from an obstinate people, the money necessary to equip and pay soldiers and sailors, to purchase munitions of war and to build costly vessels.   The proposed plan answered very well ; it was found to be simple, suave and especially easy of repetition ; it was repeated so often that, at the present time, one-third of the entire revenue of the Government is required to pay the annual interest on the debt of the nation to the fundholders.   The rise of the modern European plutocracy may be said to date from the establishment of national debts, or, ar I might call them for the sake of distinction, of government debts. The government debt of England is but the corner-stone of a larger fabric, i.e., the real national debt, which is made up not only of the capital borrowed and spent for public ends, but of the capital borrowed and spent for local and private enterprises,—an immense and incalculable sum, owed by the nation, in the main, to the plutocracy.

LONDON, *May 29th*, 1889.

As on a former occasion the mention of tailors led me, perhaps whimsically, to some passing remarks about the Jews, so the talk about capitalists and bankers, which filled up the short measure of my last letter, again leads me to speak of this peculiar people. But, this time, the connection is anything but whimsical, anything but circuitous; for in all which has to do with money, the Jew is as much at home as a scavenger in a dust-heap—so, at least, many good Christians would put it—as a bird in the air, then, let *me* say, by way of corrective, though I will frankly admit that if his way is as full of wonder as the bird's, it is certainly less full of grace. No picture of contemporary life in Europe would be at all complete that did not have in it something of the Jews; and this poor incomplete outline, which you laboriously piece together from my letters, will be somewhat clearer for the word or two which I can add regarding this strange people.

The Jew, as an individual, is not interesting

But the interest which the individual lacks is made up a hundredfold in the race. Decidedly the Jews are a remarkable, a wonderful people. Verily it may be said that they thrive by the favour of God, for of man's favour their part has been slender. . . . Prophecies have a knack of getting themselves fulfilled after a manner which would astonish no one more than the prophets themselves. May not a gifted man have keen prescience of an end, apart from adequate knowledge of the means by which the end is to be brought about? The sacred books of the Hebrews are full of the promise of power to them, full to overflowing with the conviction that they are the flower of the earth, the chosen of the Lord of life, the destined rulers of men, even to the uttermost corners of the earth. But the sacred writings are full also of weeping and wailing, of fierce denunciations of the people's heedlessness, of passionate protest against the people's sins, of menace and of warning that only chastened and strengthened by suffering and sorrow shall they inherit "the earth and the fulness thereof." Grand figures, those old prophets; now with their promises of all that is glorious, now with the rod of the Eternal uplifted in their hands! They were under absolute conviction of the vital power of their race, penetrated with its power of persistence. They felt that this intense vitality must in the end prevail, and establish them in power over other nations; and they felt all the more keenly the danger of decay to this vital force which lay in the sins and backslidings of their people.

But when the Hebrew prophets prophesied power and dominion to the "seed of Abraham," what was chiefly in their minds was the temporal predominance of their race, the political subjugation of alien races. They could scarcely dream of any other channel along which might pour the energy of their people. In the main their notion of lordship lay in political conquest. But in the nature of things the conquest of the world by the Hebrews was an impossibility. The spirit which informed their religion and moulded their conduct was from the first hostile to a tolerant attitude towards other faiths and other customs. In default of such tolerance, tribes equally insignificant in numbers, such as the ancient Greeks and Romans, would assuredly never have conquered the world and held it under their dominion. But the pre-science of power was a true one ; and now, after five-and-twenty centuries, the prophecies are being justified in a manner undreamed of by the prophets. The Jews are among the masters of modern Europe. They waited long for the tide of fortune. It came to them at last with the decay of feudalism and the growth of industry, since which time, notwithstanding all efforts to keep them down, they have steadily increased in wealth and importance, and have gathered up into deft hands the reins of power fallen from the once strong hands of the

feudal landowners. The lord-financier has dis-
placed the lord-territorial.

I have been told that the Jew is grasping, relentless, a hard taskmaster, and withal hypocritical,—
this, at least, is the opinion of a great many Christians, chiefly of those who do not know any Jews,
and who will not know any Jews because they are
grasping, relentless, etc., etc. I have myself seen
little or nothing of the Jew in person. But I have
looked on this picture; also on another. The
chief crime imputed to the Jew—beyond the first
and unpardonable one of being a Jew—is that he
is or has been the typical money-lender, the usurer.
In general, during the Middle Ages, the Jew is
represented as a usurer. The Shylock of Shakespeare is the type. But if the Jews as a class
became money-lenders and pawnbrokers, if they
betook themselves to the blind alleys and miry
lanes of industrialism, that was because the Christians shouldered them out of the clean streets and
broad thoroughfares. For centuries this people
laboured under disabilities of all kinds. They were
social pariahs, like our *Etas* and *Hinin*.[1] But their
position was infinitely worse than that of the latter.
They had no civil rights, and no protection save
that granted to them as the slaves or property of
the rulers of the lands in which they dwelt. All
honourable ways of employment were closed to

---

[1] The two lowest classes in the social constitution of old
Japan.—Ed.

them.   Princes, indeed, found them useful as a
resource in financial embarrassments, borrowed
from them, and usually dispensed with the pretentious formality of repayment.   Princes therefore
were usually inclined to treat them with some
degree of fairness ; but the hatred and suspicion
of his Christian subjects occasionally overbore all
protection the prince could afford, and on such
occasions the Jews were plundered, tortured and
put to death.   When, in later times, the Jews as
money-lenders occasionally got a Christian into
their toils, is it surprising that they in their turn
did their best to spoil the spoiler ?   It is scarcely
fair to judge of a man solely by the way in which
he treats his enemies ; we must also hear what his
friends say of him.   I have been told by fair-
minded persons that the Jews have at all times
stood by one another, and that the richer individuals of the race are quite as full of care and
charity for their poor and destitute as the rich
Christians for theirs.   I said above that the accepted
type of the Jew in the Middle Ages was the Shylock
of Shakespeare.   But although the great dramatist
holds up the Jew to obloquy and derision, his
inevitable finger is on the time's sore place.   From
out the mouth of the detested Jew himself he
hazards the lesson which it has taken so long to
learn : " He hath disgraced me, and hindered me
half a million ; laughed at my losses, mocked at
my gains, scorned my nation, thwarted my bargains,

cooled my friends, heated mine enemies; and
what's his reason?   I am a Jew.   Hath not a Jew
eyes? hath not a Jew hands, organs, dimensions,
senses, affections, passions? fed with the same
food, hurt with the same weapons, subject to the
same diseases, healed by the same means, warmed
and cooled by the same winter and summer, as a
Christian is?   If you prick us, do we not bleed?
if you tickle us, do we not laugh? if you poison us,
do we not die? and if you wrong us, shall we not
revenge?   If we are like you in the rest, we will
resemble you in that.   If a Christian wrong a Jew,
what is his humility?   Revenge.   If a Jew wrong
a Christian, what should his sufferance be by
Christian example?   Why, revenge.   The villany
you teach me, I will execute, and it shall go hard
but I will better the instruction."

"Thou shalt drive out nations mightier than
thyself, and shalt take their land as an inheritance."
This is one of the many similar kinds of promises
contained in the sacred book of the Hebrews.
Strange, almost incredible as it may appear, there
is little doubt that this prophecy is in steady
course of fulfilment.   Industrial development is
largely dependent on, and bound up with, the
skilful manipulation of credit; and in this field the
great Jew financiers have, as a body, no rivals.
This is due not merely to their skill as individuals,
but to the fact that they work in international
concert—a Jew being a Jew first, and an English-

man, a Frenchman, a German, or what not, afterwards. While making due allowance for the
prejudice, jealousy, suspicion and exaggerated
fears of Christians—especially Roman Catholic
Christians—there seem to be solid grounds for the
distrust and anxiety to which this concentration
of financial power in Jewish houses has given rise.
This power may be used, and no doubt has been
used, in bringing pressure to bear on those who
make war and peace, in supporting or shaking
national credit, in fostering gigantic enterprises the
industrial soundness of which is in the inverse
ratio of their size, and in many other ways calcu-
lated rather to profit the financial manipulators
than the world in general. But although finance
is that in which the Jew especially shines, his light
is by no means obscure in the many walks of
commerce and industry—he is prominent in all
of them, agriculture alone excepted (another proof,
if one were needed, that this people owes its
present position to the fact that the era is industrial
before anything else). The other day, I was
invited by a member of parliament to be present
at a meeting of his electors, when he addressed
them on some subject of current politics. After
the address, I was introduced to some of his
prominent supporters. Two of these I found
were rich Jews. The member of parliament told me
that his election was in a great measure due to the
influence of their wealth and position in the district.

If we go lower down in the social scale, we find no change in the signs of the time. Jews of the poorer class are sober, industrious and law abiding. I am told that in London they are now invading many trades which until recently were in the exclusive possession of the Christian population. Their sobriety, industry and thrift make them formidable competitors for employment, so that the more worthless and thriftless among the Christians are being gradually supplanted by them. If they do not " take their land as an inheritance " they take their work, their wages, and their position in the industrial hierarchy. In certain countries this advance of the Jews from high to low, as it were in a solid phalanx, has been particularly noticeable since they were put into full possession of civil rights—an act of justice indirectly brought about through the growth of industry and the popularisation of science, which, in their turn, have contributed to the evanescence of religious rancour: the greater attention of men to the affairs of this world relieving them of some of the load of anxiety concerning the future of their own souls and that of others.

Eager for gain, shrewd, quick-witted, industrious, helpful to one another, fertile in expedients and not over-scrupulous in methods of business, the Jews of to-day are what centuries of exposure to danger, contempt and hatred have made them. When one reflects over it, the history of this race is a record of marvellous endurance, a testimony to extraordinary vitality—so far as I know, without parallel or precedent. A people which has remained a people without once during eighteen centuries casting anchor on any national holding-ground; which, during the long course of its history, whether as an established nation or merely as an errant or captive race, has maintained itself separate, recognisable and peculiar down to the present day; which, while adapting itself with marvellous facility to changes of position, climate and circumstance, as conqueror and conquered, master and slave, landholder and outcast, has handed down from century to century, far back as the probe of history can reach, an unbroken series of traditions, an unchanged faith, and a ritual and customs which have outlived those of every nation on earth—such a people is well worth the attention of any student whatsoever, whether he belongs to the East or to the West. The day may not be far distant when these people will swarm to our shores. If so, they will shoulder out the Chinese and Parsïs, and it is as well we should know with whom we shall then have to deal.

LETTER XXXIV.

YASHIRI TO TOKIWARA.

Tokio, *June 3rd*, 1889.

I HAVE made it a practice, now for some years, to read the best English and French novels which I have been able to obtain; especially those which are modern, which deal with contemporary life. I recommend you, when you can spare the time, to do the same. No other kind of reading can well be more instructive and useful, provided you make your choice with care. For, after all, however high we may rate the more pretentious order of works—theological, philosophical, political, economic, scientific even (so far as science is directly concerned with man, not things)—all such works must, or should, be based on observed facts, on the actual ways, thoughts and words of men. The modern European novel professes, if I mistake not, to give an accurate picture of European society, to put it before us as it really is. The true artist, I presume, takes his stand in some section of society, in this or that distinctive order or category of men; there sets down his easel,

197

spreads out his canvas, and paints, as nearly as he can, what he actually sees about him. Provided that something, however slight, be thus authentically recorded for us and for posterity, how excellent a piece of work is there done! The great artist, of course, will be more delightful and instructive to us than the mere honest and painstaking one, for it is the privilege of imaginative insight to seize upon essential facts and group them together in such a manner that their reality shall strike us more thus than on the actual stage of the world. Great artists, however, are few and far between; we may be thankful for any narrow strip of scene, any one trait of life, faithfully presented to us. The risk to be run in this connection comes from clever work which is not honest. There are artists who let their fancy run riot, and there are also feather heads who, because they cannot endure commonplace, must needs take, and mistake, fancy for the true insight of imagination; between the two, some trivial, incomplete show of reality, cleverly decked out, assumes an ephemeral importance, and shunts the undisciplined faculties of the general along a false track—not always easy to retrace.

Some of the European novels which I have had recommended to me are of this kind—that is, works of fancy. Even to me, who am not directly acquainted with Europe, this is obvious. Such novels are often mere trial essays, sketches which the sketchers should not inflict on the public, which the public, were it wise, would not look at, or merely look at and pass elsewhither. I surmise that the public, even the well-educated part thereof, is not fully conscious of the importance of the novel. To me, a novel written by a man of true' insight appears as a document of quite infinite value : an authentic record or picture of the time and place, to be consulted with profit by successive generations of men, by thoughtful persons who desire to understand in what way, and by what means, they have become that which they are. Any true, genuine presentment of this kind is a possession conquered for us and for posterity, something snatched from under Time's all-effacing fingers, perennial in its value, for ever inexhaustible. From this point of view, even the somewhat too bestial productions of the French realistic school are not without recognisable merit. The fault which I find in the writers of this school is that they have no fit sense of proportion. We know that cesspools and sewage drains exist, but we are perhaps rather too prone to try and ignore their existence. An occasional whiff therefrom, however unsavoury, is in order : it is well to remind us that cesspools and drains require to be kept in good condition; but it is an offence to take us by the nape of the neck and forcibly hold our noses over them till we are in danger of forgetting that there are flowers and other things of sweet savour. Judging from the ascendency of this school, the number of works it produces, and the importance which is attached to them, one might almost suppose that the civilised nose of the West is becoming perverted, denuded of its healthy instincts, unresentful of the evidence of putrefaction and disease.

Biography is another kind of reading to which, with novels, I more and more incline as valuable food for the mind. On the whole, however, I am disposed to rank the novel above the biography. The biographer cannot have his hands so free as the novelist. He is fettered by the nature of his work. I may say, without paradox, that the biographer is frequently compelled to sacrifice reality to exactness. A painter would comprehend my meaning: you can record too much. A photograph is more exact than any picture, but a good picture will have in it more of the reality which we want than will the photograph. Besides, for our present purpose, pictures of contemporary life in Europe are more useful than records of eminent men.

Such novels, then, as shadow forth the essential features of social life in Europe, I would recommend to the attention of young Japan. Let young Japan collect facts rather more rigorously, and philosophise rather less ingeniously. Let our reformers study these renderings of life in the West, not with the object of slavishly imitating the Westerns, but of understanding them as they are —the good that is in them and the bad. No one can be more opposed than I am to the kind of imitation which I see about me here at the present time. Those habits, customs and idiosyncrasies which are peculiar to us, which are ours in virtue of our being Japanese, I would wish to see preserved ; they will, in fact, preserve themselves a any cost, and if we foolishly shut our eyes to the fact that we *are* Japanese, we may find the cost a heavy burden to bear. Nevertheless, if it is true that the character of a nation determines the form of its institutions, it is also true that this character is in some measure plastic, apt to receive and retain impressions from the outside world. Thus our institutions, which we have remodelled from outside, and which are the embodiment of ideas unfamiliar to us, must, by the continued presence and pressure of these ideas, tend to re-mould our national character. Having adopted the forms of Western civilisation then, let us look to the essence of it, that we may find ourselves as little as possible at cross-purposes. But in order to select and reject we must first know what *is*. Our energetic and intelligent reformers would therefore do well to make us better acquainted with the works of able European novelists. Faithful translation and intelligent comment would befit them better than much with which they are now occupied.

LETTER XXXV.

TOKIWARA TO YASHIRI.

LONDON, *June 12th*, 1889.

IN every country which can be said to be civilised, China perhaps excepted, there is a party in favour of movement and a party in favour of standing still. The one calls itself the party of progress: for putting new things in the place of old; the other the party of conservation: for keeping old things in their places. Sometimes the party of progress pulls an old thing down without having prepared any new thing to put up in its place; at other times the new thing which is to take said place is found to take it with a difference, so that in the putting up of it other old things get knocked down, to the surprise and hurt of people standing idly agape. When the conservators have the upper hand, it often happens that the roof above our heads is in danger of crumbling in. When the progressists have their way, it now and then comes about that over our heads there is no roof at all.

The coming and going of political parties, the disputing, the occasional speech, the continuous babble, the uprooting of real and imaginary abuses, the re-sowing of the seed of use and abuse : all this is very interesting to the observer of politics, as a play is interesting to a playgoer. But in the larger scene it is more than ever necessary for the actors to improve on the rude traditions of their art, to perfect their skill of mime and intonation, and, above all, never to allow the passion and conviction of real life to supplant the simulated passion and conviction of the stage. But, if the onlooker can manage to persuade himself that the show is a reality (which, indeed, is occasionally the case on disorderly stages) perhaps the most entertaining moments are when conservators, under the deepest conviction of the necessity for conserving, begin to pull down while imagining they are propping up ; or when progressists, with their eyes steadily fixed on the goal ahead of them, as steadily, though unconsciously, progress in the direction of their rear.

From the complexion which events at home wear, I perceive we shall endeavour to shape our system of government after the German rather than after the English model—a wise endeavour, I cannot but think. The English constitution, especially the system of party government, is fitted only for a nation which has arrived at maturity, when further growth, or decay, is slow. It is the

most excellent manner of grouping together law-
makers so that they shall find it difficult to make
laws, whether good or bad ; and for that reason it
is unsuited to a people in its childhood, when it is
always outgrowing its clothes and imperatively
requiring new ones to be made for it, even if ill
put together. These considerations, however, do
not deprive party government in England of interest,
even for us. So far as I have been able to understand it from a cursory examination, it appears to
have come about somewhat in the following way.
From two to three hundred years ago there lived in
England two wise men—political philosophers: the
fountain heads whence sprang the two main streams
of English political theory. By a more than usually
superior arrangement of Providence (whose greatest·
work, according to some, has been the building
up of the British Constitution) these two wise men
were not contemporary in their wisdom, although
the wisdom of the one closely followed that of the
other. Each in turn had his say, and each in turn
profoundly influenced the mode of thought of his .
countrymen. As I think I have remarked in one
of my former letters, the most remarkable example
of the power of an abstract idea concerning the
future to mould the entire life of a people is to be
found in the history of the old Egyptians ; and
perhaps the most remarkable example of the power
of an abstract idea concerning the past to do likewise, is to be found in that put forth by the elder

of these two wise men—Hobbes. But it is in the nature of things that an abstract theory regarding the future, will usually remain fixed for a longer time, and will exert a more enduring influence on a nation or race, than one which regards the past; for of the future we are for ever ignorant—an abstract theory about the future, once well ingrained, is in a position of strength, and defends itself with ease against other abstract theories. But the farther we recede from the past, the more numerous and concentrated become the beams which the light of experience throws back on it, and thus an abstract theory about the past has to do battle, not only with other abstract theories, but with the slow accumulation of concrete historical facts. So it has now come about that the ground-idea of Hobbes' political theory, which was adopted for his by Locke (the other wise man) is daily crumbling away—may be said, in fact, now to have crumbled away altogether. This is another instance of those pleasant ironies which fate always keeps in store for us—not the crumbling away of the theory, but the effect of it while it held sway over men's minds. Hobbes, who lived during the era of the Great Rebellion in England, when, as you know, that "immortal rebel," Cromwell, "hewed the throne into a block," was so persuaded of the dangers to the common weal which spring from the admission of the right of resistance in the people to the sovereign power, that he invented

the figment of the social contract, and of the complete surrender of individual rights to the power
entrusted with government, arguing at great length
therefrom the illegality of resistance.   Then followed Locke, who, desirous of showing that the
doctrine of absolute non-resistance is a fatal bar to
national progress, adopted Hobbes' ground-idea,
but improved on it by the new figment that only
certain individual rights had been voluntarily
ceded, and others retained.   Finally, the famous
Rousseau appeared as the apostle of this faith, and
gave *his* interpretation of it : the most magnificent
revolutionary sermon ever preached, a thing which
men found graven in their minds as if by magic,
and which, according to the foremost historical
students, contributed not a little to bring about the
French Revolution.   I gather that, on the whole,
Hobbes retained the allegiance of those whose
inclination is to stand still, for there seems to be
a natural correlation between the idea of absolute
authority in the king and that of immutability in
political forms.   Locke, on the other hand, was
followed mostly by the moving and removing
spirits.   But since those days a remarkable change
has come over the face of things political.   The
people has climbed up into the king's place, and
political parties, while retaining the same badges,
have in reality changed sides ; the party of progress
declaring itself as a whole in favour of the absolutism of the new power and of the surrender of

individual rights to it, the party of conservation in general opposing this tendency.   An important and interesting exception to this general rule lies in the treatment of the political problem of which we have heard under the title of the " Irish Question."   This exception is typical of certain others, which, though important enough in themselves, attract less attention and engender less heat of controversy.   It might be imagined that a political party which exerts itself to protect individual rights from invasion would rather welcome than otherwise the proposal that the Irish people should manage their own affairs locally.   But, for the moment, the master impulse of this party (which is now in power) is at all costs to preserve, if not the substance, at least the semblance of imperial power.   And this is not surprising when we reflect that the history of Europe has of late been a history of consolidation for the purposes of empire.   Within the last twenty-five years Italy, from being a "geographical expression," has grown to be a nation, and the Kingdom of Prussia has become the Empire of Germany.   Even now efforts are being made to consolidate the populations of the Balkan States.   If we look yet farther west, to the United States of America, we find that the Federal power has during the same period gained somewhat, at the expense of that of the States.

But the problem of government in Ireland is of

special interest to the student of human nature—
and on much wider grounds than those of passing
politics—for it supplies distinct evidence of the
germ of a higher, though as yet transcendental,
code of morality.   It may, I think, be taken for
granted that the nimble party of progress is usually
in the van, while the stertorous party of conservation is for the most part found in the rear, of the
march of evolution.   The party of progress has a
natural tendency to "evolutionise" more rapidly
than the other towards a higher or more ideal type.
Hence it is of the greatest interest to note that,
lately, the nimble party has in a manner leaped up
to another plane of morality, thus occasioning
surprise and bewilderment to many amiable, respectable, but slow persons.   This has come about
in the following manner. For some years past there
has existed in Ireland an association whose main
object, for political purposes, is to harass, and, if
possible, drive out of Ireland the landlords, many
of whom are tainted with the original sin of
English extraction.   An excellent means to this
end has been devised, by persuading the peasants
to band themselves in the refusal to pay rent to
their landlords.   The persuasions have been of
many kinds, ranging from the purely verbal argument to that of the leaden bullet and the poniard
point (for dull, obstinate understandings).   They
have been applied, with some success, not only to
unpatriotic peasants who insisted on paying their

rents, but to unpatriotic landlords who put a tyrannical law into execution for the recovery of said rents. Until quite recently, political parties in England were at one in condemning the object and the methods of this association. Of a sudden, however, the party of progress, marching in the van of evolution, were caught, and, as it were, whirled up to a moral platform, from which they now look down upon the other party with a not unpardonable contempt. From their elevated position they more profoundly pierce the misty steam which arises from the heat of passion and prejudice, the bounds of their moral horizon are enlarged, they have a more acute as well as more sympathetic perception of the moral bearing of words and actions. That which yet appears to others as rank dishonesty or brutal terrorism, they plainly perceive to be neither the one nor the other. As ill things sometimes wear the mask of goodness, so good things occasionally masquerade as ill ones ; but both good and ill are justified, or rather identified, in time, place and circumstance. It is well always to approach such questions with a mind largely open to conviction, else one is apt to be left behind, to find oneself in the inglorious rear of progress. The ethics of the van will evidently not be apprehended by us without strenuous exertion. It may be, perhaps, that the great mass of men will be for ages, if not for ever, incapable of attaining this ideal. This, indeed, is

14

the sorrowful and depressing opinion of an English journal of recognised standing and ability. A writer in this journal seeks to illustrate his meaning by calling to aid certain mathematical conceptions. Thus, there are in the measurement of space, or determination of position therein, certain algebraical formulæ which are held to apply to space of four dimensions, although it is impossible for us to imagine any space save of three dimensions. Similarly, without being truly able to imagine it, we may speak of two-dimensional space, and it is clear that to beings living in two-dimensional space, if we may make the supposition, any object lying outside it would not be cognisable, though perfectly cognisable to us who live in three-dimensional space. Again, any object which lay in a space of four dimensions would not be within our sphere of apprehension, but in that of beings living in four-dimensional space. We may apply this illustration by metaphor to ideas. We may speak of a four-dimensional system of morality, not comprehensible to those bounded by three-dimensional morality.

The illustration which I have thus borrowed and just set forth is ingenious ; it should therefore be regarded with suspicion ; yet it may have the merit of explaining the phenomena on which I have dwelt. But, if so, how depressing is the immediate outlook for us in this direction ! For, mark you, this higher or four-dimensional morality

is a thing which cannot be taught, since the moral
sense must first be transformed in order to appre-
hend the four-dimensional canons. The moral
sense must grow, must "evolutionise," must take
transcendental form and colour of such kind as, in
our present gross and brutal condition, must over-
top our powers of imagination. The gradual
formation, improvement and final practical acquisition of a moral instrument, so vastly improved
upon that in present vulgar use as to differ from it
not merely in degree but in kind, must require the
lapse of a great many years—I fear to think how
many. If we look at the ordinary operations of
nature in cases which may be taken as analogous,
it may be a matter of tens of thousands, nay,
hundreds of thousands of years before we reach
the desired end. No doubt the conscious selective
power which is the prized possession of man may
do much towards accelerating growth. The development of a plant, for instance, may be greatly
hastened and improved by careful selection of soil
and by discriminating and energetic application of
dung to its roots. Similarly with men: those who
are desirous (as all men worthy of the name must
be) of developing and transforming their moral
sense should proceed by parity of reasoning. They
should select a favourable habitat, some soil pre-
eminently suited for the required development;
such, for instance, as that of Ireland, or, again, that
of the South American republics. Proceeding

strictly by analogy, they should be unremitting in
the careful application, to the roots of honour and
probity, of what I may call moral manure : an
intimate   mixture   of   prevarication,   mendacity,
swindling, arson, brutal outrage, and murder.

LETTER XXXVI.

TOKIO, *June* 16th, 1889.

YOU write very much at your ease on the subject of religion. It is for you entirely a theoretical matter, to be pondered over in a spirit quite detached and quasi-philosophical. I am unable to look at it in that way. Before you lies the better part, or, at least, the greater part of life; its end appears to you a long way off, your thoughts find ample scope within its term. I, on the other hand, am so near the end of mine that my thoughts perpetually strike against the bourne ahead, and as my interest in this life wanes, so it waxes in what there may be beyond it. But, apart from the difference which in this respect marks the young from the old, there is another, still more trenchant, and more or less indifferent to youth and age, for it is the outcome of temperament. In the course of my life I have met many men, some good and some bad, to whom religion was in no way a necessity, with whom religion, while admitted as a matter which requires careful attention from the

213

intellect, was shut out from their daily lives, or simply unable to find a hold therein.   Such men are from temperament unfit to judge usefully of religion, even from an abstract or philosophical standpoint, because religion is neither abstract nor philosophical, and philosophy is nothing if it is not to influence the practice of life.   In this matter the judgment of the few—the select few, if you please—is at best but useful to themselves as an intellectual exercise ; the fruits thereof, if any, are without sap or savour for the many.

The great mass of men are not of the philosophic temperament ; their passions are strong and their desires keen-edged, their reason is weak ; they do not naturally find their happiness in moderation and the exercise of self-restraint ; the path of virtue is not easy to them,—they find it steep and rugged, for they are scant of breath and tender of foot.   Thus they require not only the most positive precepts for their guidance, but the most positive authority for the precepts—an authority beyond the reach of cavil, above the chances and changes of this life, veiled, unchangeable, inflexible in the exercise of justice, in the award of punishment to the evil-doer and of reward to the righteous.   To walk without stumbling by the light of one's own intellect is a very difficult, and, for most men, an impossible proceeding.   The circumstances of life and the conditions of men are such that not one in a thousand can thus proceed with safety.   Not only must a man be by disposition mild and equable, and of a clear intellect, but his condition in life must be such that he can find leisure for thought, for meditation.   Leisure, however, is the portion of the few.   The average man is taken up with the labour which enables him to live ; he has neither time nor inclination to meditate.   His attention is perforce concentrated on the details of life, to the exclusion of its problems ; he is glad to find these ready solved for him by authority.   If you ask him to reflect on any such problem, he looks bored or distressed ; like the aboriginal savage who, at his interlocutor's desire, attempted to fix his mind on the simplest abstract notion, he will carry his hand to his brow and declare that such matters make his head ache.

I cannot but think that you and others of our progressive school fail to attach due importance to such considerations.   I will not say to you that you judge others too exactly by what you are yourselves : that is a reproach which is too frequently and often foolishly made.   The solid structure of our judgment regarding others necessarily rests on the fundamental belief that they resemble us, that their necessities, hopes, fears, passions and desires are the same as ours.   Were it not for this belief, the world of men would be a chaos, life in common an impossibility.   Nevertheless, experience shows us that points of real dissemblance do exist among men, that no rule is so absolute as not to afford many exceptions to it. The real difficulty for any one man on any particular and important point of belief or conduct is to know whether he is therein one of the many or one of the few—or rather, to be more precise in my meaning, to know whether the mass of men are by nature and disposition capable of assimilating the particular belief or of practising the code of conduct which are natural to him. This difficulty is much more serious than people in general are disposed to allow, but it perfectly accounts for the fact that in treatises on the conduct and the beliefs of men (not on the properties of *things*) men of extraordinary ability often fall into the most astounding errors. For men of extra ordinary ability are often, from the fact itself, of an aberrant constitution. In their youth especially, before experience has forced them to observe the constitutional differences which exist between them and others, they are wholly given over to abstract and sterile generalisations, to the shaping of theories which show great ingenuity and little judgment. It takes years to teach them that points of dissemblance, however slight, are real, deep as life, and only to be abolished with life itself. Men are as jars of *saki*: like enough to one another, yet not one exactly like another, each with a defect here and an excess there which is part of itself; you could only get them quite similar by casting the lot in precisely the same mould,—but that is not the way Nature works.

Between the several families of man who people this small planet of ours, the points of dissemblance are still more marked than between the individuals of any one family, and the attempt to force all civilisations, all opinions, beliefs, modes of life and modes of thought into the same mould is a vain one. Disappointment and disenchantment await those who make it. You think that the Christian religion in one form or another is a necessary part of the development of our people. Perhaps you are right, but only on the assumption that we *can* develop freely, naturally and entirely in the European sense. The growth of the European nations has been profoundly affected by their religion, for this, together with the legacy of thought and the frame of institutions which they derive from Greece and Rome, has made them what they are. I ask myself whether the Japanese race is so constituted that it can receive from this religion the same permanent impression which other races have received. The supposition that our neighbours of the Celestial empire could be radically Europeanised is so strange to those who know them as to appear ridiculous; yet we come from the same stock, from the same family as they do. If so complete a change is impossible for · them, is it altogether possible for us ? These, however, are questions rather interesting to ask than possible to answer. Cogitations and considerations of an abstract kind are inadequate to lead us to a

conclusion upon which we may found ourselves
with safety. Never, to my knowledge, has an
experiment been tried, so fraught with great and
not-to-be-foreseen consequences to a nation's life,
as that which we are now trying—so light-heartedly
too, with so green a hope in the future, so touching
a confidence in the result. Ah me! such also was
the spirit in which was undertaken the great revo⁻
lutionary reform in Europe at the close of the last
century. How calm and serene the dawn of it;
and at noon what a darkness as of midnight, and
saturnalia of the denizens of the infernal regions
let loose upon earth! I pray to the Other Power
that our fair islands may be spared so ghastly a
sequel to the rosy dawn which gladdens the eyes
of our reformers. But the sequel I shall not see,
and on the whole I am disposed to be glad that
such is the case.

LETTER XXXVII.

LONDON, *June 26th*, 1889.

I IMAGINE that art and vulgarity do not readily consort together. It is in the nature of the vulgar mind to be not merely careless of beauty, but unresentful of ugliness. Now, the English are beyond all question a vulgar-minded people, and I find it difficult to believe that they can be artistic ; yet this is not to affirm that a vulgar people may not accomplish considerable things in the way of art, as the English undoubtedly have. Nor am I playing with paradox—a most dangerous game—as you might perhaps suppose. Are there not exotics as well as wild flowers, flowers which grow by careful training in an alien soil, and others which flourish unaided in nature, each kind beautiful in itself? I will not press the parallel too far : art in England is not precisely an exotic, but it does not appear to take root naturally and deeply in the minds and hearts of the people. Be this as it may, it has come to be a theory with me that a vulgar people cannot, as a people, be artistic. But (I imagine you asking) are the English really a vulgar people, or is it merely that their ways are not our ways, and that their ways are unfamiliar to you? I answer that, were this so, the deduction ought to hold good equally for the French and the Italians. But, as a matter of fact, I found neither French nor Italians vulgar. There is about the masses in England an outer coarseness, a surface vulgarity which is repellent to a foreigner, and which is much less noticeable in France and in Italy. But, for that matter, they are all more or less on a plane of equality as compared with our people. You would not, for instance, readily conceive the difference between a London mob and a mob in Tokio. The perfect patience, the gentle courtesy, the cheerful good-humour of our vast throngs on festal occasions, came back to my mind most vividly the other day, when, for curiosity's sake, I mingled with a London crowd on the occasion of a great mass meeting. It is not that there was bad humour, or impatience, or gross rudeness; but there was a lack of those slight courtesies, affabilities and politenesses, a disregard of the feelings of others in little matters, a pushing, shoving and self-assertion, all of which stamp a people perhaps as strong and self-reliant, but yet more assuredly as coarse and vulgar.

I must repeat again that in this people, taken as a whole, there is no sense of artistic beauty.

The dress of the lower and lower-middle classes is invariably hideous, ill fitting, disclosing no sense of the grace of form or drapery. The poorer houses are squalid, those of the rich stiff and formal. (I note an exception, however, in the case of country wayside cottages and small houses, often prettily set off with climbing plants and flowers.) But when we consider how great is· the wealth of the country, the amount expended by the people individually (and collectively by the government) on beautiful public buildings or works of art is ludicrously small. Horticulture (the culture of that which supplies artists with their most lovely designs) is not even on a plane of comparison with ours. What this people and European peoples in general admire are railway trains, big bridges, manufactories, machinery and ships ; the last not so much for beauty as for size and speed. Their big stone buildings, though not without a certain grandeur, are unfinished in detail ; the ornamentation is coarse and ill executed. (I must, however, make yet another exception here in favour of some of the churches and other buildings erected in the middle age of Europe.) Above all, what is admired over here is size ; and this is especially remarkable in the most powerful offshoot of the Anglo-Saxon race, the English Americans, who prize bigness above everything. On the whole, I take it that a Japanese cannot but look upon the great stone buildings of Europe in much the same way as a

European now looks upon the remains of Egyptian architecture—the huge pyramids, the vast temples of Louksor and Karnak, the palaces of the Pharaohs —as evidences of a barbaric magnificence and splendour which the world has outgrown.

In society I have heard many opinions expressed as to Japanese art, some of them flattering to our national vanity and some not ; many comparisons, too, between the art of Japan and that of Europe, a few of them just, many rather ingenious than just, more yet neither the one nor the other—mere babble, signifying nothing. I have listened to high praise of the miniature excellence, the ingenuity of design, the delicacy of detail, the grotesque yet graceful conceits and frolic fancies of our artists ; and again—behind a thin veil of good breeding or politeness—I have perceived the minatory form of dispraise, hesitant, gentle at times, at others severe, professorial, occasionally even truculent in bearing, more or less energetically indicating criticism of shortcomings in respect of grandeur and ideality, of the usurpation of fancy at the expense of imagination, of the degeneration of the grotesque into the burlesque, and, in fine, of the want of capacity in the brain to conceive, and in the hand to execute, the more lofty purposes of art. The praise I took with pleasure, the dispraise, I trust, with becoming humility, being anxious to gauge rather than to strive with opinion, and not unwilling to believe hat both in praise and blame, though expressed with facile and sometimes felicitous exaggeration, there lay truths worth pondering.

But, at bottom, in comparing two peoples with regard to capacity for art, the main point is generally overlooked. Yet this point is obvious enough to any one who will look about him in the two countries (Japan and England), who will cease trying to balance the excellences and shortcomings of some score individuals on either side, and turn his attention to the handicraft, the occupations, the tastes and pleasures of the masses. Such an observer cannot but come to the conclusion that, whatever may have been in the past, and whatever may be in the future, the one race as a whole now shows an artistic perception or instinct which the other does not. In our country, from high to low, from the artist to the artisan, from the court painter to the very *Moji Yaki* and *Améya* of the streets, the artistic capacity seems innate ; the instinct and power of imitation (without which there can be no backbone to art) is there. We are essentially an imitative, an assimilative people. Are we not giving the most striking proof of this in the astonishing facility with which we are now imitating European forms and assimilating European ideas— just as, 1600 years ago, we imitated and assimilated, as easily and as faithfully as was possible in days when communication with the outside world was rare and of exceeding slowness, the forms and ideas of the Chinese ?

The justness and quickness of the eye to perceive, the mingled sureness and delicacy of the hand to execute : no other basis is possible for art. The sublimer creations, as they are vaguely enough called, spring not from the education of the hand and eye, but from that of the intellect and imagination, in which very likely the Western world is ahead of us. With the growth of these is bred the desire to body forth ideas which, rooted in observation, come to flower only in the most highly cultivated minds. But such ideas are not capable of being simply, directly represented ; and thus the great artist is driven to express himself partly by the power of imitation, partly by the power of symbolical representation. It may well be that in the latter power the foremost artists of the Western world are superior to ours,—a past so rich, so full, so varied as that of Europe is an ever-green pasture-ground for the imagination,—but when we leave the artists and turn to the people, and to what constitutes the foundation of art—the spontaneous appreciation of form and colour and the skill to imitate—the case is very different. And, indeed, if we confine ourselves for comparison to England alone, the difference may be put in a single sentence. Art, in England, is the occupation of the few ; in Japan, it is the delight of the many.

LETTER XXXVIII.

YASHIRI TO TOKIWARA.

TOKIO, *June 30th*, 1889.

AN English lady who occasionally pays us a visit came to see my wife yesterday. Thereupon followed a conversation which amused and interested me. The talk was at first about the head-dress worn by Japanese ladies; then it branched off to the practice of painting the face, and to the use of the various unguents and cosmetics for accentuating beauties and dissembling ugliness. I mention the matter, which is slight in itself, because it came upon me as a first revelation of the small yet obstinate dissimilarities in the mental constitution of different races, dissimilarities such that between two individuals of distinct races mutual agreement on certain matters becomes impossible, from the simple fact that the words in which a definite idea is clothed and bodied forth by the one represent to the other a different idea, or simply no definite idea at all. This was the state of the case in the conversation between the lady visitor and my wife. Both were perfectly good-humoured

and courteous over the matter, each smiled forth
friendly appreciation of the other's views and sentiments, but it was plain to me they were standing
on either side of a rift in the ground too wide for
either to step over.   I brought a little plank of my
own and laid it across, but the rift was deep and
I could see their heads turn at the bare idea of
crossing.

My wife, as you can guess, was all in favour
of the native customs ; her visitor entirely, though
not obstinately, opposed to them.   Accustomed
as I am, from long practice, to European modes
of thought, I had no difficulty in following our
fair friend's arguments.   Thus, with regard to the
head-dress, she admitted the grace and picturesque
effect of it, but contended that, inasmuch as the
make-up of it is too long and intricate a work for
daily repetition, and therefore necessitates the use
of the narrow Japanese wooden pillow at night,
in order that the fabric shall escape injury, we
sacrifice comfort to appearances.   My wife fully
admitted the charge, but could not perceive the
gravamen of it.   Nothing more natural than the
standpoint of each lady.   A race of people in whom
the æsthetic sense is undeveloped will naturally
estimate the sacrifice of bodily comfort to mere
appearance a folly—nay, even a kind of insincerity
and pretension.   An artistic race, on the contrary,
will incline for its pleasure rather to the picturesque
than to the comfortable.   In this regard, indeed,

we may penetrate a little deeper and remark that in one and the same word—comfort—will be embodied ideas of varying complexion : so wide the variation, in this case, as to preclude mutua. understanding.

The conversation then turned on the merits and demerits of calling in the aid of art to supplement the handiwork of nature in the female face. I was not altogether surprised to hear that, in the English mind, it is a matter of reproach to any woman that she should paint her face. For my wife, the reproach appeared only merited if the painting were ill done. " A woman who is clever enough to improve her looks by artificial means and does so," said she, " deserves commendation, not reproof." " Well done or ill done," replied the' foreigner, " you trample the natural under foot of the artificial." " You must permit me to remark," I broke in, " that this is precisely what civilisation is ever engaged in doing : what is considered artificial at one stage grows to be thought natural at the next." " And then," added my wife, " what matter whether the thing done is natural or artificial, provided the thing is good ? " But here our friend withdrew into the regions of the philosophical and abstract. " You must admit that the practice of deception is in itself dangerous, even where the particular deception practised is innocent. The moral sense is a delicate instrument with an edge easily turned or blunted by careless usage.

The habitual use of paint and cosmetics, too, argues the waste of much time at the toilet table, to say nothing of the encouragement it gives to female vanity."

All this was thrown away on my wife. For her it is the business of a woman in easy circumstances to look pretty and to display charm. It is the only return she can make to the world for the easy time the world allows her. As to the charge of deception she answered, rather neatly: "You do not practise deception by adhering to a general custom, but by stealthily departing from it. Did all men habitually lie, you could deceive only by telling the truth." We all smiled, and my wife, in great good-humour, proceeded to make tea in the unceremonious manner we use with strangers. There was some little more sparring between the ladies, on the subject of women staining their teeth black on getting married; but the sparring was more in sport than ever, for my wife seemed disposed to admit that there is a good deal to be said against the custom,—from which fact I gather that that serpent, young Japan, has been whispering in her ear.

LETTER XXXIX.

LONDON, *July* 10*th*, 1889.

I SEND you photographs of several monuments
and buildings of London. Among them you will
see two which I have marked with a cross, and
which stand not far from where I am at present
living. The large round building is called the
Royal Albert Hall of Arts and Sciences; the
other, which looks somewhat like a temple, is the
Albert Memorial, so named because it was erected
after the death and in memory of the Queen's
husband, Duke Albert of Saxe-Coburg and Gotha.
The Hall, too, was named after him, he being a
distinguished patron of the arts and sciences.
In the Memorial the figure of the Prince, seated
within the four columns, is plastered with gold
over all, by which proceeding was lost the opportunity of a happy contrast between the rich ornamentation of the monument and a simple marble
figure of the man in whose honour the building
was erected. It may be that the artist, with that
Western tendency to symbolism which I noticed

when I last wrote, privately proposed to himself to satirise the age, in the form of one of its leading personages, by thus symbolising the subordination of all things, including the artistic sense, to the general and indefatigable pursuit of wealth. But symbolism leads us far afield, and not infrequently as far astray. Yet I reject the notion that anything in these two buildings which may offend the sense of beauty is due to mere want of taste in the artist or in his patrons, for on reflection I find good reason for supposing that, apart from the obvious purpose of each edifice, there is a symbolical meaning attached to each and to the two taken together. Of the Memorial I have just spoken. The Hall, as you perceive, is round; which, being an unusual shape for a hall, probably symbolises the circle in which the arts and sciences are perpetually turning, now the arts and now the sciences facing the rising or the setting sun. The association of the two monuments in symbolism will be at once perceived on recollecting the Western institution of the marriage-cake or bride-cake. I do not know whether you have ever seen one of these cakes, which are often highly and elaborately ornamented; but if in imagination you place the Albert Memorial on top of the Albert Hall, the two will resemble nothing more than a gigantic bride-cake, which may be accepted as symbolic of he happy and prosperous married life of the Queen and the late Prince. A little practice very soon improves the power of perceiving allegorical meanings, a power which grows with the general expansion of the faculty of imagination. This faculty of imaginative, and sometimes imaginary, construction displays in these lands a freshness, a vitality, a buoyancy which charm and elate, stand you never so solidly on guard against seduction. Nowhere is this more so than in the dusk and dusty domain of archæology, where the very air you breathe is witchery and fascination. Here the Western archæological explorer, laying down his pick and shovel in the shade of an old tomb, or by the broken columns of an ancient temple, will read you in these, and in the ruined potsherds and battered tablets at his feet, the story of a nation's life and of a people's beliefs.

In the Eastern nations generally, the tendency of individuals to vary from one another, to develop in different directions, is not marked. It is, at all events, less marked than among the leading nations of the West, where there exists in the individual a more pronounced desire towards free development of his special capabilities, and in society a greater freedom to that end. Thus it is that nearly all branches of human activity bear a finer fruit in the West than in the East. There is a neater and more general adaptation of special means to special ends. There is no cause for surprise, then, that a people which, like the English, lacks artistic capacity, should nevertheless turn out some very respectable works of art. However inartistic a people may be as a whole, there will be found artistic individuals in it; and, given the freedom and capacity to develop, there will be found an artistic class within the' nation, but apart from it. The same observation holds of music, and I can illustrate it without fear of race bias by a comparison made within the area of the West. Thus it is a most common experience in England to hear and read of "the musical public," meaning thereby that portion of the public which cares for music. In France and Italy the analogous expression is not met with; nor is it known, I am told, in Germany, —at all events in none of these countries is there an expression of the kind in common use, the public at large being itself "the musical public." Nevertheless music flourishes in England, and some very respectable work is done in it. My ear is not attuned to Western strains, but I remember being much struck with a little incident during my trip to Rome. —— and I had stopped for one day in a small town on our way to the capital. After dinner, in the cool of the evening, we strolled out with an Englishman who had been eating at the same table with us. Turning round the corner of a street, we came upon a crowd surrounding three small boys who were playing music on stringed instruments. We stood there listening for some little time. At last the Englishman said: "Now, you might go round to every little town in Italy and

find in every one of them three small street boys
who can play as these do; and you might hunt
round all the small towns in England and not
find one street boy such as these among the lot:
that is one difference between a musical and a non-
musical people." Substitute Japan for Italy, and
the plastic and delineative arts for music, and you
will have a ready-made comparison to hand.

So I notice that if anything is to be done, built,
made in England, which, by common consent,
requires artistic treatment, the thing is done well
enough, provided the artist be given a free hand.
The public say : Give the artist the requisite money,
and let him do the right sort of thing. This the
public say and do, because they believe it to be
creditable and proper ; they do not in the least
care about the matter personally, but they have
heard of the " educative influence of art " and
such-like phrases, and they believe that they can
encourage art simply by putting their hands in
their pockets now and again. In all other cases,
where there is no direct, or, as I might call it,
official connection, between art and the thing to be
done, the natural indifference of the people to beauty
asserts itself, and ugliness or dulness reigns. Outside of painting a picture and moulding a statue
there is no art here. Decorative design is known
as an expression of what might be, but is not; at
best, what there is of it is copied from bygones, and
unintelligently set amid alien surroundings, or is

made to do duty in the place of something more appropriate and natural to the occasion or the subject. Take their coins, for instance. Next time the opportunity occurs, examine the English gold piece, the sovereign, where, on the reverse of the coin, the national legend of St. George and the Dragon is depicted. The figure of St. George is noble, the action of the steed is full of beauty and fire. Both, in all probability, have been copied from, or suggested by, some antique model. But the lack of artistic power to adapt the borrowed material to the circumstances of the case is at once evident. Mark the unreality of the conception. St. George is armed with a sword some eighteen inches long. He cannot by any possibility reach the Dragon with it. Of this he is aware, for he holds the sword well back out of the way. Finding himself in this dilemma, St. George, with the disciplined heroism of a brave man in a moment of supreme danger, disconcerts the Dragon by trying to ram his right foot down the Dragon's throat. The Dragon is evidently taken by surprise. St. George, profiting by the momentary indecision of his foe, probably, I take it, kills the Dragon by driving his right spur (which the artist has omitted to depict) into the animal's brain. In Japan, this maleficent, overgrown scorpion would have been hunted up by a nimble boy and knocked on the head with a stick.

LETTER XL.

YASHIRI TO TOKIWARA.

TOKIO, *July 14th*, 1889.

I SAID in a former letter that, for certain reasons, I am inclined to believe that the evils which vitiate the industrial organisation of society in the West may possibly touch us with less corrosive effect. What I had in my mind was the probability that the Western freedom—I had almost said licence— of individual industrial effort, the undisciplined protrusion of commercial aims and ideas into all departments of human activity, would in our case be met to some extent by the socialistic bias which, I think it must be admitted, marks the character of the Japanese people. If we compare our past feudal organisation with that of Europe, we may see that at all, or nearly all, points of departure from similarity of direction, ours is in that of socialism, or of ideas whose natural sequence approximates thereto. It is only by re-cognising that this spirit permeates all classes of the nation that we can understand how the radical change in the tenure of land which followed the

Restoration was at once possible and natural, able to be brought about without the wreckage, violence and plunder which have accompanied similar changes in European countries.

It is plain, however, that, even in Europe, the industrial organisation of society will not be per. mitted to rest peaceably on the basis of individual liberty within the present limits of Western law and custom. Some kind of compromise will have to be effected between individualism and socialism. But in Europe the industrial organisation has grown up permeated and informed by the individualistic idea; its structure has attained a certain degree of rigidity which will make the necessary readjustment difficult and possibly dangerous. While socialism is in Europe as yet in the theoretical stage, a matter for discussion, for intellectual inquiry, its spirit is with us a part of the national temperament, germane to the character of the people. Hence we may expect that, so far as we are concerned, socialism will seize hold of and to some extent mould the organisation of industry, and that we may be spared some of the flagrant abuses with which the Western system is at present overweighted, and the danger which would be incurred in the necessary attempt to rid ourselves of them.

The incessant demonstrations of European social-istic agitators, and the equally incessant putting forth of new programmes by social theorists, are evidence of more than transient dissatisfaction with the present social structure. At bottom they are half-unconscious protests against the persistent application of an old order of forms to a new order of things. There is a confused perception that the mass of laws, customs and usages which have grown up, and have been devised to regulate with what smoothness was possible the relations between individuals and classes of a community, are no longer in good working order, either because ill applied, or because smooth application is no longer possible; the relations themselves having grown other than they were. Now, one of the most important ends which society proposes to itself, in establishing and enforcing these manifold regulations, is the safeguarding of itself from the damage to which the gathering-up of the reins of power into unworthy hands would expose it, be these the mailed hands of the robber, the deft ones of the charlatan, or the forceless ones of the fool. Society instinctively recoils from, and seeks to guard against, the danger which threatens it in the association of power with violence, irresponsibility, or folly. To the best of its ability, it endeavours to establish tests by which worth shall be recognised and entrusted with power. As a guarantee of its right use, society, by force of law or force of opinion, attaches responsibility to power wherever it can. But, as the constitution of society alters, as it grows from one stage to the next, power passes or tends to pass from one set of men to another set; or, from changes in organisation or in circumstance, new powers appear, to the wielders of which society is at a loss how properly to affix duties or responsibilities.

The more closely we consider the present condition of the social body in the West, the more plainly we perceive the growing importance of the power of the purse, and the efforts, unsuccessful as yet, which are being made to affix responsibility in the use of it to those who wield it. The statesman, the landowner, the soldier, the lawyer—nay, even the manufacturer and the merchant—each of these, exercising the power which is entrusted to him, feels that he is in some measure responsible for its right use. But the mere purse-holders, whose summed-up millions are invested in securities or lent out at interest, do not, as a body, feel themselves responsible to society for the manner in which these millions are used. There are two forms in which this irresponsible power of the purse bodies itself forth. Against one of these the socialist sets himself to organise a new force, a league of labour, just as disregardful of the general interest, as irresponsible to society, as the force it opposes. But while the world is thus looking on, not without anxiety, at the deploying of the hostile forces of capital and labour, its attention is withdrawn from the other form, more subtly pervasive, in which the power of the purse, regulated or not, is profoundly to influence the world's future.

The development of trade, of commerce, of the

industrial system generally ; the thousandfold application of inventions and apparatus for turning the
same amount of man's labour to greater account,
doubling, trebling, quadrupling the mass·of its production—at the lowest computation swelling the
volume of this production at a rate far exceeding
that of the growth of population—this must be
attended with one of two chief results : Either the
entire population must benefit by the distribution
of the increasing produce, or the increase must
go to a certain number of individuals in so great
abundance that, being unable themselves to con-
sume their share entirely, they will lend the sur-
plus to others who can make profitable use of it :
that is, a class grows up, as you point out very
clearly in your letter of May 5th, which lays the
nation under tribute—in other words, the capitalist
class is created. Very likely both these results
enter into the reality ; but the latter result seems,
from this distance at least, to be the more striking
and important.

The power of capital, the modern power of the
purse is, as I have already remarked, of two kinds :
one, obvious to all men with bodily eyes and ears ;
the other less so, obvious only to men with understanding. Of the first—coercion of labour, met
by counter-coercion of capital—there is abundant
evidence ; society meanwhile looking on anxiously
thereat, in the vain hope that it will not be called
upon to interfere in order to preserve the com-

batants and itself from ruin.   Of the second—
secret, subtle, unrecognised fully even by the
wielders thereof—I would now speak a word, if
perchance I may make myself understood.

In your letter of May 5th, you do not, in so
many words, say that the purse-holders, great and
small, have laid the nations under tribute ; but, in
essence, that is your meaning. The entire class
of capitalists, those who live and grow on the
accumulated savings of the past, have in effect
lost—as you point out—the faculty of re-entering
into possession of their capital, but they have
retained that of varying its distribution. In essence
it comes to this : that the purse-holders have exchanged their capital against a definite annual
command over the labour of the community, labour
to be directed to the production of whatsoever the
purse-holders shall desire. Possibly you have not
reflected fully as to what meaning is in this ; what
it connotes of power, yearly increasing, in the class
of which we speak—power to do good or to work
evil, according to the direction which this labour is
forced into ; power to direct men's lives into clear
channels or foul, to turn men's hands to fine work
or coarse, healthy work or unhealthy, life-giving or
death-dealing, precisely according to the desires
of those in whom this terrible power lies. It is
a power which, according to its use, will have in
it the making or marring of a nation—unless the
nation awake to this fact, and regulate the use of

it by affixing responsibility to the user. And what in likelihood, will be the unregulated desires of such a class? We can guess but too well: French cooks and finery, with whatever else is necessary to make these serve: the fungus upgrowth of a household varlet class, choking the good grain of honest, healthy labour; a class which apes, yet despises its masters, and robs them the while with expectation of one day taking their place; over-fed, insolent, a worse than useless burden on the back of the nation: a multitude of grooms and coachmen, harvesting disease or gathering the seeds thereof in the miry streets, under the midnight rain, at the door of the fashionable entertainer of all kinds: a further multitude of ministrants, whose ministry, especially in such circumstances, is not of the healthiest—tailors, milliners, needlewomen, perfumers, hairdressers and the like; necessary, indeed, in that men and women need to be dressed (the more gracefully the better, not forgetting, however, that much grace lies in simplicity), but, under these conditions, drawing heavily on the national reserve of health-giving occupation in order to trick out puppets who cannot even plead the sole justification of puppet existence: the amusement of the public.

What is this outline which I have just sketched? Naught else but a freehand, perhaps somewhat exaggerated, copy of what the genuine European novelist and biographer have shown me as already

16

existing. Only, the European novelist and bio-grapher, following their true vocation, paint what *is*; do not greatly concern themselves with how this came to be, nor with what this is likely to become. The direct, immediate, palpable effects on society of a class which is plutocratic and nothing else are visible enough to these writers. It is a common-place of moral as of natural philosophy, that stag-nation is the breeding-ground of corruption, and that corruption spreads by contact. But there is a mildness of manners and a diffused spirit of tolerance which first accompany the growth of material prosperity, and which make the time re-dolent with treacherous promise. The sunshine of material prosperity, too, dazzles the human owl, makes gold to glitter the more, until scarcely anything else can fix the attention.

In the expenditure of the rich lies the justification or condemnation of their existence in the state. The English political economist, John Stuart Mill, showed, in his book on political economy, that he was on the track of this conclusion when he drew his distinction between expenditure laid out on productive and on unproductive labour; but the political economy of his day is a meagre field to till in; and, in truth, this distinction of Mill's is of no practical value,—I do not even admit it to be valid in theory. All labour is productive. The question rather is: productive of what? Wealth or *ill*th? health and life, or disease and death? calm

content, or purulent desire? Beside this distinction all others fade into the trivial or the inane.
To the body of purse-holders the conventional
moralist and the conventional political economist
preach charity, but their respective definitions
thereof are wide as the poles asunder. Let the
puzzled purse-holder nevertheless take heart of grace.
He can, if so he chooses, render invaluable service
to his fellows,—but then he must learn to set store
less by French cooks, tailors and ballet-dancers,
than by landscape gardeners, artists and the
Cinderella of Western fable.

LETTER XLI.

TOKIWARA TO YASHIRI.

LONDON, *July 24th*, 1889.

YESTERDAY, as I was walking along a large thorough-fare crowded with people, I beheld a sight which set me a-dreaming. A small, inconspicuous, unimportant object, or series of objects, to gaze on, yet not insignificant. You know that in Europe, and especially in England, the art and practice of advertising have been extraordinarily developed. But I must tell you that here in London, over and above the ordinary means of advertisement afforded by the newspapers, and by the placarding of hoardings and vacant wall spaces, there is a custom of hiring poor work-less ragged men as perambulating advertisement boards, especially in connection with theatres, concerts, circuses and other forms of amusement. Each man carries two boards, hanging from the shoulders, one down the back, the other down the front of the body. On these boards are pasted the notices. The men are called "sandwich" men, a "sandwich" being an article of consumption which consists of a slice of meat laid between two slices of bread, usually dry and unpalatable. Over and above the mere outside resemblance, the unpalatableness of the edible perhaps suggests the name given to the man, it being a saying here that "life would be tolerable but for its amusements," and another saying that "an Englishman takes his pleasures sadly." Indeed, I may say, in confirmation of these two sayings, that most Englishmen look as if life were rather a burden to be borne than a boon to be enjoyed. But this is by the way. What particularly engaged my attention was, that at the tail of a string of these "sandwich" men were three or four of them whose advertisements consisted of extracts culled from the sacred writings of the Christian Bible, such as "God is love," "Sin no more," and others of a like kind. This struck me as so curious that I asked an explanation of it from an English acquaintance. "Yes," he said, "you have fallen here upon a trait which is peculiar to our people : an ever-present tendency to the vulgarisation of religion. What you saw to-day is but one instance among many of the persistence of this tendency. Not only is it the custom in many private houses to hang upon the wall texts taken from our Bible, but even in public places, such as the waiting-rooms of railway stations and the parlours of public inns, nay, even in certain places which I need not more particularly describe, you may see such texts suspended on the walls

for the edification and sanctification of the people.
On Sundays, in the public streets, the parks, the
squares of the metropolis, you can listen to the
monotonous delivery of ignorant and vulgar,
though often earnest men, on the most sacred
subjects. On occasion, but more rarely of late
years, well-meaning persons will accost you and
inquire into the state of your soul; they will pro-
vide you and your household with specially printed
matter on the subject of salvation, and this without
any desire or encouragement on your part. If,
from the circumstances of your life, you are in any
way thrown in with this kind of persons, you can
rarely lay your hat down for a few moments without
finding a printed leaflet or two in it on taking it
up again; in going out of your house you will
probably find a tract on the door-sill. The slovenly
men and draggle-tailed women who parade the
streets in orderly mobs, with flying banners and
brass bands, form part of a vast association which
gives itself the name of the 'Salvation Army.'
Many, perhaps the majority, of these people are
animated with a real desire to bring religion home
to the mind of the masses, but the methods which
they pursue are very questionable. To advertise
a divine mystery or a golden rule of conduct in
the same manner as, and in juxtaposition with, the
programme of a music hall, is to supply matter for
jest to the satirical and for grief to the wise. To
demonstrate with band and banner in the cause of

religion precisely as you demonstrate in the cause of teetotalism, or for the removal of an obnoxious tax, is to place religion by invidious comparison on a level of relative paltriness. The power of religion lies in its appeal to the personal and mysterious, and in its dissociation from the common aims and methods of life. The way of these people is to vulgarise and unsanctify it."

Thus spoke my friend; but, as I have said, the sight of these men parading biblical texts in the streets had set me a-dreaming, and my friend's voice was as the voice of a dream echoing from a hollow world of unreality. What real meaning was to be attached to these singular phenomena, these religious street-orations, park meetings, distributions of tracts and Bibles, marchings, counter-marchings, and songs of " Salvation " regiments? I judge that the religious sense, under whatever forms it may show itself, is native to the English people, perhaps in much the same way as the artistic sense is native to our own. After the necessary business avocations and trivial relaxations of life, religion claims a large share of the attention of the people; they are interested in it, they busy themselves with it, much as we busy ourselves with flowers, gardens and things of beauty.

It is also a noticeable thing that, however incompatible vulgarity may be with art (I speak not of individuals but of nations), it is by no

means incompatible with religion.   No doubt, a
nation may be religious without being vulgar, yet
religion appears to thrive on vulgarity.   At the
present moment France, the most artistic of the
Western nations, is at the same time the least
vulgar, the least religious, and probably, the
least moral.   For morality, which in the ordinary
judgment of men is closely associated with religion, seems likewise to be at home with vulgarity and at odds with æsthetics.   Judged by
the comity of civilised nations, I have no doubt
that we should be pronounced to be on the whole
a somewhat immoral and licentious nation—as a
matter of fact immorality is well-nigh the only
serious fault which European critics find with us—
and, indeed, do we not admit the impeachment ?
do we not profess to be in search of a basis of
morality and religion ? do we not discuss these
matters with that calmness which denotes indifference ?   Westerns have gone out of their way to call
us a highly artistic race, but the word "vulgarity"
has never been whispered in connection with us.

Consider, again, what we know of the ancient
Greeks and the ancient Hebrews, the two races
which, the Roman excepted, have most contributed
to form the conduct, belief and ideas of the
European stock.   Would· it not be a tolerably
correct and compendious judgment to say of the
Greeks that they were penetrated with the idea,
saturated with the sentiment of beauty, profoundly

persuaded of the value of art as an element in human life, relatively indifferent to the value of morality, and attached to religion for the sake of the ideas of beauty which it inspires rather than for that of the code of conduct which it prescribes? On the other hand, should we not say of the ancient Hebrews that to matters of religion and moral conduct they attached the highest importance, and that art for them was of value only in so far as it might be made to subserve the ends of religion and morality?

It seems, then, that there exists a kind of natural opposition between art on the one hand and morality and religion on the other. And, as the vulgar and the artistic sense tend mutually to exclude one another in the same race, we may say that there is a kind of natural affinity between vulgarity and morality, and also, though less marked, between vulgarity and religion.

LETTER XLII.

LONDON, *August 9th,* 1889.

AMONG those who take an intelligent interest in the doings of the world at large, there are not a few who look Japan-ward; some, indeed, on the tiptoe of expectation concerning the upshot of our plunge into the sea of European methods—whether we shall come up head first or tail first. Withal, the interest evinced in us is apt to be here and there of the semi-incredulous, semi-humorous kind. You may occasionally see articles and paragraphs in the London journals the very headings of which denote a serio-comic appreciation of the changes which we are now undergoing—headings such as "The Japanese in search of a Religion," or "The Japanese in search of a Basis of Morality," and others of the sort. It cannot be denied that the collocation of the words, as they stand in such sentences as these, tickles the sense of the comical and humorous. But in the things themselves there is nothing comical whatever. We are doing that which no nation has ever yet done or ever attempted seriously to do—an entirely new, original, strange thing; without precedent in history, without sanction save in common sense. It is true that this may well move men to wonder, but only fools to laughter.

What is there in all this which is truly suggestive of the ridiculous? Nothing, that I can discover. We are recasting the constitution and the laws of our country after a model supplied to us by Europe. Very good. But laws and constitution are the verbal embodiment, the legal sanction, of custom, of use and wont. Hence, for a change in law and constitution to be effective, there must be a corresponding change in the habits and customs of the people. But the complete sanction of the habits and customs of a people (partly embodied in the law, partly in a host of extra-legal conventions), is nothing else than the religion and code of morals of the people. Religion, morality, law, custom are inevitably interdependent—not rigidly connected each with the others, of course, but so connected that if you introduce sweeping changes in any one of them, you naturally and surely awaken ideas which will bring about modifications in the others. Nothing, then, is more natural than that young Japan should find herself "in search of a religion, of a basis of morality." The fact, indeed, is evidence that the change which the country is undergoing is a real change, probing deep, and by no means a merely verbal one.

The persons who smile at the efforts of the Japanese to recover their bearings in morals and religion are entirely at sea with regard to our national character. They have no adequate conception of the extraordinary mobility and versatility of the Japanese mind. In any European country, so complete and swift a substitution of the new for the old would have been attended with violent social convulsions. No Western theory of social evolution could warrant the doing of that which we have done and are yet doing. Nothing short of practical success could justify it in Western eyes—wide open now at the undeniable practical success which has followed. Yet, had people in this part of the world given but the slightest attention and consideration to the events which followed the restoration of the Mikado, they would have been well prepared for what has taken place in the last few years. History, I imagine, furnishes no parallel to the action of our three hundred feudal nobles in 1869. The spontaneous abandonment of their fiefs, feudal power and military splendour, as well as their acquiescence in the subsequent arbitrary measures for commuting their incomes, stand out as most astonishing facts in the eyes of the West.

The truth is that the Japanese mind is a fertile soil for the sowing of ideas; these take root therein and come to flower with rapidity and vigour. In this respect, again, there is a strong likeness between the French and ourselves. Of all European populations the French is that most readily moved by ideas, and by these lifted out of the rut of routine and precedent. The great Revolution, you will say, affords good proof of this. I admit that to be so; I will even admit that France has suffered more through the faults of the Revolution than it has gained by the sweeping aside of abuses. Ideas are luxuries, and luxuries are costly, sometimes to excess. Nevertheless they are the sole means by which nations save themselves from slavery of one kind or another. Thus, if I understand the English people at all, I should say that from the beginning of this century, or at least from the end of the Napoleonic wars until within some thirty years ago, this nation was suffering from a dearth of ideas, it was on the road to slavery under the demon of utilitarianism. That part of man's nature which thrives on ideas was becoming atrophied; the nation had put *things* into the saddle and was being ridden to death, was falling into spiritual torpor. The man who first helped to arouse it was Thomas Carlyle; but he shouted himself hoarse before he was listened to, save by a very few. As to the French people, the unfortunate thing for them at the time of their revolution was that the men of action, of practical knowledge, of ability in the management of men and affairs, who should have carried out the ideas which permeated the nation—these men were non-

extant; the *ancien régime* had stifled them. A
number of amiable, well-meaning and intelligent
men met together to rearrange the affairs of the
nation. They had some knowledge of what ought
to be done, but how to do it was beyond them.
The doing fell into the hands of the only men of
action extant—the nameless rascals and hardy
scoundrels whose appearance is inevitable directly
the bonds of order are at all loosened, but who are
promptly put out of the way by business men.

NOTE BY THE EDITOR.

THE correspondence between Tokiwara and Yashiri ends here somewhat abruptly—at least in the translation, for there is no lack of further material in the original. After some hesitation, I deemed it judicious at this point to bring the publication of the letters to a close—at all events for the present. My hesitation is natural enough : for if, on the one hand, I fear to weary the reader more than I dare hope to interest or amuse him, on the other, in the disclosure of this fear, I risk to mortify my Japanese friends. On one or the other of the horns of this dilemma I must elect to be impaled : in choosing the latter, as I now do, I may at least hope, by showing consideration for the reader, to obtain the salve of his indulgence.

H. B.

PRINTED BY
HAZELL, WATSON, AND VINEY, LD.
LONDON AND AYLESBURY.